A BITTER END

THE EB EATS DINER MYSTERIES

POPPY BRIDGEMAN

Ebook ISBN: 978-1-990509-82-7
Paperback ISBN: 978-1-990509-83-4

Cover created by Getcovers

FREE BOOK

Use the QR code to claim your copy of Burned by BLT when you sign up for my newsletter learn how Eliza became so determined to clear her name.

1

I checked the temperature on the slow cooker for the third time in ten minutes. The green chili pork had been braising since four a.m., filling EB Eats with smoke and cumin and roasted poblanos. Steam rose when I lifted the lid, and my mouth watered despite the early hour.

"Still not ready," Anthone said from behind me.

I turned to find him kneading masa for tortillas, his hands working the dough in steady rhythm. Dark circles shadowed his eyes—he'd probably slept even less than I had.

"It's ready," I told him. "You're just nervous."

"Amalia Limonete doesn't do second chances." He shaped a ball of masa and pressed it between his palms, testing the consistency. "One bad dish, and I'm the guy who ruined Nueva Vida's reputation."

"You're the guy who makes the best posole I've ever tasted." I pulled two mugs from the shelf and poured coffee for both of us. "Besides, she's just one person. There will be hundreds of people at the festival today who'll love everything you make."

"Right. One person whose review could make or break —" He stopped, shook his head. "Sorry. I know I'm obsessing."

The front doorbell chimed. Through the kitchen window, I saw George Kramer walking toward the counter in his usual rumpled suit, that cop alertness he never quite turned off even when he was off duty.

"I'll get it," I said, grateful for the distraction from Anthone's spiraling.

George smiled when he saw me, but it didn't reach his eyes. "Morning. Got a minute?"

"Always." I poured him coffee without asking—black, no sugar, the way he'd taken it every morning since I opened EB EATS. "What's wrong?"

"Nothing's wrong. I just wanted to check in about the festival." He looked at the coffee in his mug like it held some kind of message. "Security's arranged, first aid station's set up, but with crowds that size, things can get chaotic. You'll have your phone on you?"

"George." I kept my voice gentle. "I've run the diner through tourist season. I can handle a food festival. I know it's not a rousing endorsement, but the death at the food fair last season was nothing to do with the vendors."

"I know you can handle it." He looked down at his coffee. "I'm not trying to—I just worry."

The care behind his concern made my chest tighten. Before I could figure out what to say, the door chimed again.

Vic Simons walked in carrying a toolbox and wearing that easy confidence that seemed to follow him everywhere. His eyes went to George, then to me, taking in the moment without comment.

"Eliza," he said. "Brought that extra folding table you needed. Want me to set it up in the tent?"

"That would be perfect." I tried not to notice George's jaw tighten. Vic was my other... admirer sounded too Victorian, but boyfriend candidate sounded weird. He'd volunteered his days off from firefighting duties to help with the festival. "Thank you."

"No problem. Anything else you need help with before things get crazy?"

The difference hit me. George asked what could go wrong. Vic asked what I needed. Both meant well, but the contrast made something shift in my mind.

"Just the table," I said. "We're under control here."

Vic nodded, flashed that quick smile, and headed back out. George watched him go, then set down his coffee.

"I should get back to it," he said. "But if anything feels off today—"

"I'll call. Promise."

After he left, I stood at the counter for a moment, listening to Anthone's knife work on the cutting board and the low simmer of the chili. The morning light through the windows painted everything gold, and for just a second I let myself enjoy the quiet.

"Was that Vic?" Anthone called from the kitchen.

"Yeah. Bringing the extra table."

"Hmm." The tone suggested he'd noticed more than I wanted him to. "You know, if you ever want to talk about—"

"Nope." I grabbed my coffee and headed back to the kitchen. "We have tortillas to make. And Jacquie will want her kitchen back soon enough.

BY NINE A.M., the town square had transformed. Vendor tents lined the walkways in neat rows, their white canopies bright against the blue New Mexico sky. Strings of paper flowers crisscrossed overhead, and the scent of roasting chili mixed with sweet churros and grilled corn. I'd been surprised at the number of food events that happened every year. Once a quarter might be excessive, but each had a different focus. This one came with a contest.

I was arranging our display when I heard the voice.

"Absolutely not. The lighting here is atrocious."

A woman stood in front of the New Sunrise Café tent, arms crossed, surveying their setup with the expression of someone who'd just discovered expired milk. She wore all black despite the heat—tailored pants, silk blouse, designer sunglasses pushed up into silver-streaked dark hair.

Amalia Limonete. I recognized her from her author photo, though the pictures didn't capture the way she commanded space just by existing in it. She kept the business in the family, using her nephew to do all the video for her show.

"Ms. Limonete," the café owner stammered, "we followed the guidelines—"

"Guidelines are minimums, not targets." She circled their booth, examining everything. "If you're serious about this competition, you need to consider angles, presentation, the customer's sight lines. Your signature dish is in shadow."

A younger man appeared at her elbow, camera in hand. "Aunt Amalia, the light's good if they shift the table six inches left."

He raised the camera and clicked off a few shots, then showed her the display. She studied the screen, her expression softening.

"Knox has a point," she said. "The shift might work."

I watched Knox Thorne help the café owner reposition their table, his movements efficient. He couldn't have been much older than thirty, with the kind of lean build that suggested nervous energy kept him moving. When he smiled at his aunt, it reached his eyes—genuine affection without the wariness most people showed around Amalia.

"All the vendors arranged by eleven?" Amalia asked him.

"That's the plan. I'm documenting setup for the festival committee." He adjusted his camera strap. "Want to see the shots from the north entrance?"

"In a moment." She turned to the café owner. "Better. Now let's discuss your garnish presentation."

I focused back on our own booth, arranging the menu cards Kashvi had helped design. Behind me, Anthone was setting up the warming trays with the same precision he brought to everything in the kitchen.

"She's not that scary," I told him.

"Says the woman who didn't just get evaluated." He straightened a napkin that didn't need straightening. "Did you see how she looked at their setup?"

"I saw her nephew suggest a fix and her listen." I stepped back to check the sight lines—not because Amalia's criticism had merit, but because it did make sense. "That counts for something."

Knox appeared at our booth, camera raised. "Mind if I get a few shots? Trying to capture the variety before the crowds arrive."

"Go ahead," I said.

He circled our display, crouching to get different angles, focused on his work. The camera looked expensive—professional grade, with a lens that probably cost more than my phone, which is the only camera I have.

"You're Eliza Burton, right?" he asked, lowering the camera. "EB Eats?"

"That's me."

"Aunt Amalia mentioned your diner when she was planning the festival route. Said you're one of the few places in Nueva Vida worth photographing." He grinned. "From her, that's high praise."

"I'll take it." I watched him review the images on his camera screen. "How long are you in town?"

"Just through the festival. I work in Albuquerque, but Aunt Amalia asked me to document this one personally." His expression shifted, something worried flickering across his features before he smoothed it away. "Family obligation and all that."

Before I could respond, Amalia's voice cut through the morning air.

"Knox! The lighting's changing. We need those vendor portraits now."

"Duty calls." He raised the camera in a small salute. "Good luck today. Your setup looks great."

I watched him return to his aunt, who launched into a lecture that required her to point out every detail in sight, including the clear sky. Whatever tension I'd glimpsed had vanished—when he looked at Amalia, he just seemed like a nephew who cared about his aunt's success.

"Fifteen minutes until opening!" someone called across the square.

Anthone appeared at my elbow, surveying the crowd forming at the entrance. "Ready?"

I looked at our booth, at the food we'd spent hours preparing, at the morning light making everything golden. At Knox photographing the festival. At Amalia reviewing vendor arrangements with standards that would make the whole event better, whether anyone admitted it or not.

"Ready," I said.

. . .

THAT NIGHT, I sat on my porch with Macchiato curled in my lap, watching the last light fade from the sky. The festival had been everything I'd hoped—steady crowds, enthusiastic responses to our food, Anthone's tension easing into confidence.

Tomorrow, the real judging would begin. Amalia would make her rounds, and the whole town would hold its breath.

I scratched behind Macchiato's ears, listening to her purr.

"Just one more day," I told her. "Then everything goes back to normal."

If I'd known what was coming, I might have stayed on that porch and never gone back.

But I didn't know. None of us did.

So when my alarm went off at four the next morning, I got up and went back to the kitchen, ready for whatever came next.

2

Anthone had been in the kitchen since dawn. The prep station was spotless, the spice rack organized, the stainless steel gleaming. He'd been braising the pork shoulder since five a.m., checking the temperature every twenty minutes.

"Sweet potatoes are hand-cut to specification," he said, more to himself than to me. "Garnish is prepped. Crema has the right tang." He wiped his hands on his apron. "What if she hates fusion? What if she thinks I'm disrespecting both traditions?"

I set down my coffee. "Anthone, half our regulars have been begging me to put this dish on the permanent menu. You've been working on it for months."

"But she's Amalia Limonete."

Through the front windows, Main Street was transforming. Paloma Santos directed the banner crew, her clipboard both schedule and weapon. A golden retriever tangled himself in every rope while his owner tried to look responsible but would have been better to put the effort into training.

Near the festival coordination tent, a young man with a camera was documenting the setup. Worn jeans, vintage band t-shirt, intense focus. Something about how he held himself made me wonder who he was watching.

The bell chimed.

Amalia Limonete walked into EB Eats like she was conducting an inspection. Tall, severe, silver hair pulled back tight. Her eyes cataloged everything—counter height, lighting, salt shaker placement. That leather notebook was already in her hand.

"Ms. Burton." Her voice carried authority. "I understand you've prepared something for evaluation."

Anthone appeared from the kitchen before I could respond, his face pale but his voice steady. "Ma'am, I've developed a Southwest-Asian fusion for the festival. Would you care to try it?"

She made a face that told us what she thought about fusion. It wasn't joyful; more like she'd smelled something foul.

I stepped in. "Anthone has been working on this for months. It honors both traditions while creating something new."

"I see." Amalia settled onto a counter stool. "Describe what you've created."

Anthone straightened. "Hand-cut sweet potato fries topped with Chinese five-spice braised pork shoulder, finished with lime-cilantro crema, pickled red onions, and toasted sesame seeds. The pork marinates overnight with local Hatch green chili, soy sauce, and traditional spices."

"Ambitious for a festival setting." Amalia pulled out a small camera. "Proceed."

Anthone disappeared into the kitchen. I heard oil heating in the wok, vegetables hitting hot metal, the rhythmic knife work. Through the pass-through, I watched him work.

"How long has he worked for you?" Amalia asked, producing reading glasses.

"About a year. He's recently started school in Albuquerque, but he understands Nueva Vida. Born and raised here. He wants to be his own boss some day."

"No ice," she said when I set down the water, pushing the glass aside.

I fetched a fresh glass, filled it with room-temperature water. This woman's reputation hadn't mentioned obsessive control over details, but watching her work, I understood why she'd built such a career. Nothing escaped her.

"Experimentation with regional cuisine can be dangerous," Amalia said, making notes. "People are protective of their traditions. Combining them requires mastery of both."

Before I could respond, the door opened, and a man strode in. Medium height, warm brown skin, groomed beard, bow tie the color of paprika. What caught my attention was Amalia going rigid.

"Amalia." His voice was sweet but no one would miss the force behind it. "How delightful to find you here."

"Rajan Okoye." She somehow made his name into a sneer.

The temperature dropped. The few customers who'd braved the crowds for their usual morning routine stopped eating. Even Bill Foster lowered his newspaper. This was better than his afternoon soap operas.

"I was hoping we could discuss tomorrow's coverage," Rajan continued, leaning against the counter. "Perhaps coordinate to avoid duplicating efforts."

Amalia's laugh could have cut glass. "I'm quite certain

our approaches will be different, Rajan. After all, we do have different standards for quality journalism."

The words landed hard. Rajan's expression didn't change, but his knuckles went white on the counter.

"Of course." His tone suggested poison. "Your reputation for thoroughness is well-known. Though I wonder if readers might appreciate a more balanced perspective on Nueva Vida's culinary scene."

"Balanced." Amalia set down her pen. "Is that what you're calling your work now? How refreshing to see you've developed a brand."

"At least my brand doesn't rely on destroying small businesses for sport." Rajan's voice had lost its honey. "But then, you've always preferred making examples rather than connections."

"Making examples." Amalia's tone could have frosted windows. "You mean maintaining standards? Yes, I suppose that would seem foreign to someone whose critical analysis involves counting Instagram likes."

Rajan straightened. "You know what your problem is, Amalia? You mistake cruelty for honesty. There's a difference between high standards and using your platform to settle personal scores."

"Personal scores?" Her eyebrows rose. "You're projecting, Rajan. Just because your own work is driven by spite doesn't mean the rest of us share your motivations."

"Spite." Rajan's voice rose enough that Jacquie looked up from wiping tables. "This from the woman who destroyed—"

"Careful." Amalia interrupted him in mid-word. "I'd hate for you to say something actionable. Though I suppose that would give your career the attention it's been desperately seeking."

The silence was sharp. Rajan's jaw worked as if he were restraining himself from speaking. Finally, he turned toward the door.

"Enjoy your preliminary tastings, Amalia. I'm sure they'll be very enlightening." He walked out.

After he left, Amalia sat still for a moment, then returned to her notebook as if nothing had happened. But her hand shook when she picked up her pen.

That was when Anthone emerged from the kitchen, carrying his creation. The plate was simple white ceramic, but what it held was beautiful—golden-bronze sweet potato fries cut by hand, each one distinct. The braised pork shoulder gleamed with its lacquer of green chili and soy, the meat so tender it wanted to fall apart. Pickled red onions added bright purple against the lime-green cilantro crema, and toasted sesame seeds crowned everything with that nutty brown that meant someone had watched them every second in the pan.

The smell hit me first—sweet caramelized pork meeting earthy green chili, bright lime cutting through rich fat, the anise note from Chinese five-spice dancing with cumin and coriander. Comfort food that had been to culinary school and come back with ideas.

"Your fusion creation," I said, setting the plate in front of Amalia.

Amalia photographed the dish from three angles. She lifted her fork, cut through a sweet potato fry and a piece of pork together, included crema and pickled onion, then brought the assembled bite to her mouth.

The silence stretched. Anthone stood frozen at the pass-through. Jacquie visible over his shoulder pretending to focus on pancakes.

Amalia chewed, her expression revealing nothing. She

swallowed, took a sip of water, cut another bite—this time with different proportions, testing the balance. Another pause.

She set down her fork and opened that leather notebook.

"The sweet potato preparation demonstrates competent technique," she said, writing. "Good texture, appropriate seasoning, proper frying temperature. The pork shows proper braising method—the meat yields without falling apart. The green chili integration is more thoughtful than I expected."

Coming from Amalia Limonete, this was high praise. I could see Anthone trying not to grin.

"The five-spice is measured correctly," she continued. "Easy to overpower, but you've let it complement rather than dominate. The crema provides acid balance, and the pickled onions add textural contrast." She took another bite, this time including more sesame seeds. "The sesame is toasted properly. Most cooks burn them or don't toast them enough."

Anthone's face was transforming.

"However." There it was. "The portion size is problematic for festival service. This belongs on a dinner plate with proper utensils, not in a paper container with a plastic fork. The components will separate, the crema will slide off, and your balance will be destroyed before it reaches the customer."

She paused, studying the dish. "You'll need to reconsider your service method. Perhaps layer the fries in the container with pork between each layer, so every bite includes all components. Or serve the crema separately for people to add themselves."

I jumped in. "The festival pricing is fixed—the net profit

goes to charity, which means we need to keep the food costs down without losing quality. We're using compostable containers because of environmental requirements."

"Ah." Amalia made another note. "That changes the economics. In that case, your ingredient cost management is impressive. This pork shoulder is expensive protein, even in bulk. You're making it work within tight constraints, which shows practical business sense alongside culinary skill."

She took another mouthful, finishing nearly half the plate. "The fusion concept has merit," she said, her tone softer. "With refinement, this could be a signature dish. The technique is sound, the flavor combinations are thoughtful rather than trendy, and you understand both culinary traditions you're drawing from."

Anthone looked like he might float away.

"However—" Amalia set down her fork. "Fusion cuisine requires mastery of both source traditions. You have solid fundamentals, but don't let ambition exceed your foundation. Master each technique independently before combining them. Otherwise, you risk creating confusion instead of innovation."

The criticism was gentler than her reviews suggested she was capable of, but it still landed with weight. Everything she said he needed to do, Anthone had done. He didn't seem to notice. He just smiled and nodded.

"I should continue my rounds," Amalia said, gathering her things. She paused, looking at Anthone. "You have genuine talent. That's rare. Don't waste it trying to run before you can walk."

After she left, Anthone slumped against the counter. "She liked it," he said. "I mean, she criticized it, but she ate most of it and said the technique was sound."

"That's probably the closest thing to a rave review she's

ever given," I agreed, though my mind was still on that confrontation with Rajan Okoye. Whatever history those two critics shared was personal and toxic enough to make Rajan lose his composure.

The lunch rush kept us occupied, but I kept glancing through the windows as Amalia made her rounds. She emerged from Dunes Cafe looking like she'd tasted something questionable—which, knowing Alistair's tendency to over-salt when nervous, she probably had. The new wine bar held her attention longer.

Then I spotted her outside the festival booths, having what looked like a heated discussion with a woman I didn't recognize. The stranger was petite, with tattooed arms and purple streaks in her dark hair. Even from this distance, her body language screamed fury.

Kashvi appeared at my elbow. "Who's that?" I asked.

"Keiko Nakamura," Kashvi said, settling onto her favorite stool. "She's working the Pueblo Kitchen booth for the festival."

The name rang a distant bell. "Local hire?"

"Oh honey, no." Kashvi had that tone. "She used to have her own restaurant in Albuquerque. Amazing place called Lotus Garden—pan-Asian fusion, ironically enough. But it closed about five years ago."

Through the window, Keiko's hands were moving in sharp, angry gestures. Amalia stood still, that leather notebook already out. Whatever was being said, it was going on the permanent record.

"What happened to the restaurant?" I asked, though I was getting an uncomfortable feeling about the answer.

"Food critic destroyed it," Kashvi said. "Came in and murdered the place in print. Called it cultural appropriation masquerading as creativity and said Keiko had no business mixing Asian techniques." She paused. "One guess who wrote that review."

My stomach sank. "Amalia Limonete."

"Exactly. Restaurant closed three months later. Martha told me Keiko had a breakdown afterward—lost everything, struggled with addiction, disappeared from the food scene. She only showed up here last month, working prep for barely above minimum wage."

I watched Keiko storm away, purple hair streaming behind her. Amalia stood watching, then made more notes.

"Going from restaurant owner to prep cook," I said. "That has to hurt."

"Martha says it gets worse. After the restaurant closed, Keiko lost her apartment, her marriage fell apart. Disappeared for three years. She's been clean for two years now, trying to rebuild. She's only thirty-one."

Something cold settled in my chest. Yesterday, when I'd overheard Amalia arguing with someone—what if it had been Keiko?

"And that's not even the best drama," Kashvi said. "Hugo Delacroix is having a meltdown about the festival."

"The French place?" I'd driven past Maison Delacroix a few times—the kind of restaurant where they probably charged twenty dollars for three asparagus spears.

"That's the one. He's been telling anyone who'll listen that the festival is beneath his standards. But get this—Amalia requested a private dinner at Maison Delacroix as part of her coverage."

Through the window, I could see a tall man in an expensive suit having an animated discussion with Paloma near the coordination tent. Even from this distance, his gestures suggested fury.

"Let me guess," I said. "That's him, and he's not happy."

"Hugo's been planning this elaborate tasting menu for weeks. Ordered special ingredients, probably spent more on wine pairings than most people make in a month. And this morning, Amalia's assistant calls to cancel. Some excuse about scheduling conflicts with tomorrow's festival coverage."

I watched Hugo's movements. The way he held himself —rigid, controlled—as if waiting for the next unwanted change to destroy him. Professional pride like that didn't take humiliation well.

"But here's the interesting part," Kashvi said. "Martha heard from someone who knows his sous chef that Hugo used to work with Amalia. Way back, before either of them was famous. There's history there, and it's not good."

"What kind of history?"

"Nobody knows for sure, but the sous chef said Hugo keeps a file—actual physical file—of every negative thing Amalia's ever written about his cooking. Going back twenty years. That's not normal."

Through the window, Hugo was still gesturing at Paloma, his movements getting sharper. Then he turned and walked away.

"This festival is shaping up to be more complicated than anyone planned," I said.

"Wait for this," Kashvi said. "Some television producer showed up this morning demanding meetings with Amalia. Word is she's been harassing every food critic within a hundred miles, trying to get content for her show."

A woman in a power suit walked past the window with aggressive strides. Her red hair caught the afternoon light.

"That's Octavia Beaumont," Kashvi said. "From some cable food network. She's been making rounds all morning, trying to corner Amalia for an interview."

"How do you know all this?" I asked.

"Martha's on the festival committee, plus the hotel desk clerk is dating her nephew. Between the two of them, she knows what everyone had for breakfast." Kashvi grinned. "Small-town intelligence networks are efficient."

Around three o'clock, when the lunch rush had died, and I was restocking napkins, a young woman with long dark hair and enough jewelry to stock a boutique walked in. Her phone was already out and recording.

"Excuse me," she said. "I'm Birdie Castellanos from Southwest Foodie Blog. I heard the famous Amalia Limonete ate here during today's tastings? Could I get a quick interview about your experience?"

The phone pointed at my face made me feel like prey.

"I'm sorry, but we don't discuss our customers' dining experiences," I said.

"Come on," she said, lowering the phone. "Just a tiny sound bite about what you made to impress her. My fifteen thousand followers are dying for insider content about the festival. This could be amazing exposure for your restaurant."

The entitlement in her voice set my teeth on edge. "We're good on exposure, thanks."

"Seriously?" Birdie's smile had an edge. "You know Amalia Limonete could make or break this whole festival tomorrow, right? My coverage could help control the narrative, but only if I have actual content to work with."

"Have a nice day," I said, turning back to my napkin restocking.

After she left, I watched her through the window, already recording herself talking to her phone while gesturing at EB Eats. Whatever she was saying probably wasn't flattering.

The afternoon wound down with its usual rhythm, but I couldn't shake the feeling that tomorrow the festival was going to be memorable for the wrong reasons. Amalia had been in Nueva Vida less than two days and had already upset a surprising number of people:

Rajan Okoye, whose professional rivalry had turned personal and toxic.

Keiko Nakamura, whose entire life had been destroyed by one review.

Hugo Delacroix, who'd been planning an elaborate dinner only to have it canceled at the last minute, with what sounded like twenty years of resentment behind his fury.

Octavia Beaumont, desperate enough for content that she was harassing people.

Birdie Castellanos, worried enough about her influencer career to get pushy about access.

Tomorrow would put all of them in the same place at the same time, centered on a woman who specialized in making enemies.

3

The back door hit the frame hard enough to rattle the dishes. I looked up from the green chili stew to see Kashvi, eyes wide.

"You need to close early," she said. "We're doing research."

I glanced at the clock. Seven thirty on a Thursday evening, festival prep tomorrow at six. "Kashvi, I've got—"

"I just heard something." She set her phone on the counter. "And if I'm right, tomorrow's festival is going to be a disaster."

Anthone emerged from the walk-in cooler with containers of prepped vegetables. "What kind of disaster?"

"The kind where someone gets destroyed by a food critic who specializes in it." Kashvi was texting. "I'm calling Jet. We need to head to The Open Page right now."

Twenty minutes later, we'd locked up and gathered at Kashvi's bookstore. She'd claimed the best reading chairs and set her laptop on the coffee table. The place smelled of old books and vanilla candles.

"Okay." I settled into the leather chair Kashvi kept threatening to reupholster. "What did you hear?"

"I was at the hardware store picking up festival supplies when I saw Amalia on her phone in the parking lot. That woman does not believe in inside voices."

"What was she saying?" Jet asked.

"Something about unfinished business and people who think they can hide in small towns." Kashvi opened her laptop. "The part that got me was when she said I found her."

My stomach sank. "Her who?"

"That's what we're finding out." Kashvi pulled up a search page. "Amalia Limonete, food critic. Let's see what happens when I add restaurant closures."

I moved beside her as the results loaded. The first article made me wince.

"The Death of Sage and Smoke: How One Review Ended a Rising Star's Career," Anthone read.

Kashvi clicked through. The article showed a restaurant interior—exposed brick, modern art, gorgeous open kitchen. And a photo of the chef: a Japanese-American woman arranging dumplings garnished with green chili and micro-cilantro.

"That's Keiko," I said.

"Read this." Kashvi scrolled to the review. "Just the highlighted part."

I read aloud: "'Keiko Nakamura's Sage and Smoke represents everything wrong with fusion cuisine—a chef who doesn't understand the cultures she's appropriating, playing dress-up in someone else's kitchen with techniques she hasn't earned the right to use. Her dumplings are technically competent, which makes her cultural theft all the more troubling."

"That's not a review," Jet said. "That's an execution."

Nobody spoke for a moment.

"How many others?" I asked. "How many restaurants has she destroyed?"

"Let's find out." Kashvi created a new search. Within minutes, we'd found the pattern.

Tucson: closed. Flagstaff: bankrupted. Phoenix food truck: owner quit cooking.

All of them had received reviews that went past criticism into attacks on the chef's identity, training, right to cook certain foods.

"She doesn't just review food," Anthone said. "She decides who deserves to cook."

"Look at this one." Jet pointed to an older article. "Portland, eight years ago. Amalia opened her own restaurant and—oh."

The review was brutal. Another critic had written: "Amalia Limonete talks a better game than she plays. Her restaurant is all concept and no execution, proof that knowing how to criticize food doesn't mean you know how to create it."

"Her restaurant failed," Kashvi said. "Closed after ten months."

I thought about the woman who'd walked into my diner yesterday—composed, authoritative. But under that, I could see it now.

"She's passing it on," I said. "Every chef she destroys is because someone destroyed her first."

My phone caught my attention. Text from an unknown number: *Mrs. Burton? This is Knox Thorne, Amalia's nephew. Could we talk? I think there are things you should know about my aunt.*

I showed the message to the others.

"Fascinating," Kashvi said. "Ask him to come here."

While I texted back, Anthone scrolled through more articles. "There's something else. Look at Amalia's social media. She posts photos of every meal, and she's specific about her food."

I leaned over. The Instagram account was food photography, but Anthone was right—the captions were detailed.

"Poached salmon, but I always order without the dill sauce. Can't stand bitter flavors."

"Perfect risotto, though I never finish the last few bites—too rich."

"Strawberry tart, but make sure to request no almonds. Severe allergy."

"She broadcasts everything," Jet said. "Allergies, preferences, portions."

"And her assistant probably knows even more," I added.

Kashvi searched. "Cleo Fontaine. Three years as Amalia's assistant. You want to know someone's habits, ask the person who manages their calendar and orders their meals."

The front bell chimed. A young man peered through the window—mid-twenties, messy brown hair, Amalia's amber eyes but sadder.

"That's Knox," I said.

He stepped inside, hesitant. "Thank you for meeting with me. I wasn't sure who else to talk to."

"Sit." Kashvi gestured to the empty chair. "Want coffee?"

"Please." He sat down, looking at our laptop and notes. "You're researching my aunt."

"Trying to understand her," I said, passing him a mug with the sugar bowl. "Why she came to Nueva Vida, what she's planning."

Knox turned his mug while he thought. "She's here for

the festival. But more specifically, she's here for Keiko Nakamura. She tracked her down."

"How do you know that?" Jet asked.

"Because I helped her do it." Knox stared into his coffee. "Two months ago, she asked me to search social media for any mention of Keiko. She wanted to know where she'd gone after Sage and Smoke closed. I found a photo from Nueva Vida—Keiko serving dumplings at last year's autumn market."

"And you told Amalia," I said.

He nodded. "I didn't think much of it then. Aunt Amalia always said she tried to give people second chances, to see if they'd learned from their mistakes. But after I told her about Keiko, she started researching your food festival. When she got the invitation to judge, she called me. She sounded triumphant. Like she'd won some battle I didn't know about."

Kashvi typed notes. "You sound like you know your aunt well."

"I'm the only family member who still talks to her." Knox shrugged like he was at the end of his options. "My mom won't speak to her after what happened with my dad's restaurant. Most of my cousins cut her off. But I kept thinking if someone stayed close, she might change. Or at least I could warn people."

"Is that why you texted me?" I asked. "To warn us about Keiko?"

"Partly. But also because I saw how Aunt Amalia was looking at your chef today. That expression she gets when she's found a new target."

Anthone went still.

"Your fusion dishes," Knox said to him. "She was taking

notes. Lots of them. After you left, I heard her on the phone with her editor, pitching a piece about cultural appropriation in Southwest cuisine."

"But she praised him?" I said determined to make sure Anthone remembered. "Besides, his grandmother was Korean. His fusion cooking comes from her recipes combined with where he grew up. That's not appropriation —that's his life."

"I know," Knox said. "But Aunt Amalia doesn't care about truth. She cares about the story that gets attention. Controversy sells."

"Why are you telling us this?" Jet asked. "Why warn us about your own aunt?"

Knox was quiet. When he spoke, his voice was soft. "Because I'm tired of watching her destroy people. My dad lost his restaurant to her review, and it broke something in him. I've enabled her by staying silent. I can't do it anymore."

How had I mistaken her enthusiasm for Anthone's dish?

"There's something else," Knox said. "Aunt Amalia's been visiting someone at the inn. I saw her coming back from their room yesterday evening. She looked like she'd been crying."

"Do you know who?" Kashvi asked.

"No idea. But whoever it is got to her in a way I haven't seen in years. She looked vulnerable."

After Knox left—with promises we'd keep him updated but not reveal him as our source—we sat in the quiet bookstore.

"So," Jet said. "We've got a critic who destroys chefs for revenge, a disgraced chef she tracked across states, and some secret relationship that makes her cry?"

"What we need," Kashvi said, closing her laptop, "is to

stick together tomorrow. All of us. We watch each other's backs and everyone who gets near Amalia."

"And maybe," Anthone said, "I cook the best dish of my life. Make her appropriation angle look stupid when people taste what I've created. For the final tasting."

"Now you're talking," I said. "Your food speaks for itself."

4

Festival morning arrived with perfect weather for an outdoor event. The sky stretched deep blue overhead, the morning air sharp and cool enough that I wrapped my hands around my coffee mug. October gets chilly, but by afternoon we'd be in t-shirts.

After three weeks of Anthone practicing his fusion dish in his sleep, and yesterday's encounters with our food critic, everything was happening today. The festival. Tonight's formal tasting where Amalia would deliver her verdict on Nueva Vida's culinary offerings.

By nine-thirty, I was caffeinated, dressed, and walking down Main Street.

Holy green chili.

The street looked like a southwestern food festival should look. Adobe-style booths matched our town's architecture. *Papel picado* banners fluttered between buildings. Someone had strung lights in the cottonwoods for tonight. The air smelled like charred chili, fresh masa on tortilla grills that I'd learned were called comals, barbacoa that had been cooking since yesterday, and somewhere nearby, churros with cinnamon.

A mariachi band tuned up near the main stage. Food hit hot griddles with a sizzle. Vendors called out samples. Children ran past already sticky with the juice from ice pops. Families claimed picnic spots while food bloggers took photos. The crowd moved between booths with the energy of people who'd been waiting weeks.

"Eliza! Come over here." Paloma Santos waved me over to the coordination tent. Her silver hair was caught up in a bandana that said "Festival Boss Lady" in pink letters.

"This is unbelievable," I said. "How did you—"

"Thirty-seven years of church fund raising and three pots of coffee," she said. "Plus everyone wanted this to work. We've got twice the registration we expected. Word got out about Amalia Limonete."

My stomach tightened. "Speaking of whom..."

"*Ay, Dios mío.* She's been evaluating since eight this morning. Very thorough."

Through the crowd, I spotted silver hair and that leather notebook. Amalia moved through the booths like she was conducting inspections, spending exactly the same time at each station, taking notes. The other judge, Rajan following in her wake, tasting and chatting without making notes.

To the side. Knox set up and tore down his equipment with every new booth. That must be incredibly tiring, and marginally useful. I watched him circle a booth serving tamales, crouching to capture steam rising from corn husks, then standing on a chair for an overhead shot. Then his aunt snapped her fingers, and he stepped in line to the next station.

"He's been great," Paloma said. "Between Knox and Rajan, they've calmed down everyone Amalia insulted.

That explained why vendors looked comfortable around him. Knox wasn't just some photographer at a food festival —he was his aunt's spin doctor.

Our booth looked like a magazine cover. Anthone had the setup perfect—our corner location showed off both the cooking area and gave us good sight lines. The menu board featured his Korean-New Mexican fusion alongside our regular favorites.

"Ready for the big day?" I asked.

"More than ready." Yesterday's nerves had shifted into focus. "Tonight, at the formal tasting, I get to have a real conversation with someone who understands food."

"Good thing Jacquie and Will are managing the diner," I said. "It's nice to worry about one thing at a time."

"Eliza!"

Kashvi's voice carried across the crowd. She'd set up what looked like mission control—folding chair, cooler, enough snacks to survive a siege. Jet was helping her and I couldn't help think that they were generals camped out on a rise to command a battle.

"Mobile gossip headquarters," she announced. "If we're going to watch Nueva Vida make culinary history, we might as well be comfortable."

"And well-informed," Jet added. "Kashvi's already gotten the morning intelligence from Martha."

"Oh, honey." Kashvi settled into her chair. "If you thought yesterday was intense, Amalia's been busy today. Three incidents just this morning, and that's only what Martha witnessed."

"She told Javier his mole tasted uninspired—which made him so mad he started yelling in Spanish. Then she informed Maria that serving *sopapillas* with honey was historically inaccurate. And just before you got here, she asked Rosa if she understood the difference between authentic and appropriation when it came to Navajo fry bread. And Rosa is married to the chief."

I winced.

"Also," Kashvi continued, "Knox has been following her around all morning with his camera. Got some interesting shots of people's faces when she delivers her verdicts. Not sure if that's going to be great publicity or evidence for lawsuits."

"Or something he's holding over her." Anyone could start and Instagram or TikTok account.

I glanced across the crowd to where Knox was photographing Amalia at a red chili stew booth. He captured not just the food, but the interactions—the vendor's nerves, Amalia's focus, the onlookers. Professional work with an eye for drama.

The morning moved with a strange rhythm—beautiful weather and crowds on the surface, while underneath, tensions simmered.

I was watching Anthone plate samples when I caught sight of a woman with red hair making her way through the crowd. She wore designer sunglasses and moved with the confidence of someone used to getting what she wanted.

She headed straight for Amalia, who was examining artisanal salsas. I'm not too ashamed to admit I moved closer.

"Amalia. Darling!" The woman's voice carried across the festival. "What a wonderful surprise!"

Amalia looked up. Her face shifted through several emotions before settling into professional neutrality. "Octavia. I wasn't aware you were attending."

"Oh, you know me—always hunting for the next big

discovery." Octavia Beaumont—I recognized her from Kashvi's research yesterday—positioned herself so Amalia couldn't escape. Her smile was wide and warm but her shoulders were tense. "Speaking of which, I've been trying to reach you for weeks. About the show."

"I received your messages." Amalia's tone was icy enough to freeze water. "All seventeen of them."

"Then you know what an opportunity this is." Octavia moved closer, lowering her voice, as if pretending their conversation was private—her voice still carried. "Your own series, complete creative control, the kind of platform that would make your book launch—"

"I'm not interested in being made into a television personality."

"But think of the reach! Think of what you could accomplish." Octavia's professional smile was cracking. "We're talking prime time, major network, the resources to really expose the issues."

"I expose fakery through journalism, not entertainment."

"Amalia, please." Now Octavia's voice held desperation, though she tried to mask it. "At least consider it. The pilot's already greenlit, we've got funding, promotional campaign designed—we just need you to sign on. Without you, the producers will kill the project."

There it was. Octavia wasn't just interested in Amalia; she needed her. Badly enough to track her down at a small-town food festival.

"I'm sorry you've invested without securing your talent first," Amalia said. She didn't sound sorry. "But my answer hasn't changed. I have no interest in becoming America's Toughest Food Critic or whatever your marketing department dreamed up. There are plenty of other people who would sell themselves to you."

She threw a pointed glance at Rajan before she turned back to the salsas.

Octavia stood there, her professional mask slipping to reveal something harder. When she spoke again, her voice had lost its warmth.

"You're making a mistake. This industry has a short memory for critics who think they're too good for mainstream success. Two years from now, when your book is remaindered and your followers have moved on, you'll wish you'd taken this chance."

"Perhaps," Amalia said without looking up. "But at least I'll still have my integrity."

Octavia walked away, her heels clicking sharp and fast. She pulled out her phone, her gestures angry as she started what looked like an intense conversation.

Knox had photographed the whole thing. When Octavia left, he lowered his camera and made a note in a small notebook from his vest pocket.

"That looked intense," Kashvi said, nudging my elbow and handing me a bottle of water.

"Octavia needs Amalia for a TV show," I said. "Badly enough to follow her here and make it sound like she wasn't stalking her."

"And Amalia just burned that bridge." Kashvi watched Octavia disappear into the crowd. "That's what, the fourth person today who's walked away looking like they wanted to commit murder?"

She meant it as a joke. Neither of us laughed.

The afternoon sun climbed higher. The festival hit its stride. The crowd thickened, vendors found their rhythm, and the air grew heavy with a dozen different cooking traditions happening at once. By two o'clock, everyone had stripped down to t-shirts, and the shade under the cottonwoods was packed.

I was helping Anthone with a rush when I noticed a commotion near the far end. A young woman with streaked hair and an armful of bangles was talking to Amalia.

"—essential that I get an interview for my blog," the woman was saying, her voice high and nervous. "My followers are engaged with authentic regional food, and your perspective would add so much credibility—"

"I don't give interviews to food bloggers," Amalia said.

"But I have over fifty thousand followers! And my engagement rates are phenomenal—I could really help amplify Nueva Vida's reputation." The blogger—I recognized her. Birdie Castellanos. Her blog, The Taste of Home, was fun. Right now, her hands shook. "Look, I've prepared sample questions, and if you could just spare fifteen minutes—"

"Ms. Castellanos, I'm familiar with your work."

Birdie's face lit up. "You've read my blog?"

"I read everything relevant to the food industry. Including your piece last month where you claimed a restaurant's ambiance was more important than technical execution and that sometimes authenticity matters less than the story." Amalia's expression could have soured milk. "Those opinions are precisely why serious food journalism has been diluted by amateur voices who prioritize entertainment over accuracy."

Birdie paled. "I—that's not what I meant—"

"You encouraged your followers to support a restaurant despite minor consistency errors, because the chef had a compelling immigrant story."

"Home cooks aren't consistent—"

"That little fact doesn't change poor judgment." Amalia closed her notebook. "If you want to be taken seriously as a food writer, develop actual standards instead of chasing social media engagement with pretty photographs and emotional narratives."

Birdie stood frozen, phone still in hand. When Amalia walked away, the blogger's eyes were bright with tears she was trying not to shed. She disappeared into the crowd, shoulders hunched.

"Yikes," Jet said from our booth. "She just destroyed that girl."

"Over a blog post," Kashvi added. "I mean, yes, Birdie's stuff is fluffy, but she loves food and she's helped local restaurants get business. Did Amalia have to be that brutal?"

I didn't answer. Part of me understood Amalia's point—consistency was important in a restaurant. If that chef was promoting home made as his brand, then Birdie had a point. But the delivery had been cruel, and Birdie was just trying to make her way in a competitive industry.

The festival continued. But I was noticing something. Amalia was leaving a trail of damaged pride and anger everywhere she went. Each interaction seemed designed not just to critique but to wound.

Around three, I noticed a man in his forties examining the vendor booths with nerves. Felix Kowalski, produce and meat vendor according to the festival information. We didn't use the big vendors, preferring to support local people. I didn't know his reputation.

He was talking to an older woman I didn't know who's booth was filled with honey is various forms.

"The quality is exceptional, really, and the pricing is competitive for the region. I think you'll find our distribution network can get your products into stores throughout the Southwest—"

"Felix." Amalia's voice cut through his pitch. "Still peddling questionable produce to unsuspecting chefs."

Felix went pale, then flushed. "Amalia. I didn't realize you were here."

I watched Knox slip into the crowd, and Rajan turn to taste the wares in a nearby booth.

"Clearly. As usual you've done no research." She turned to the honey vendor. "I'd recommend thorough due diligence on Mr. Kowalski's company before signing anything. His distribution operation has an interesting history with health inspections and contamination."

"That was one incident years ago, and it was resolved—"

"Three incidents," Amalia corrected. "Over four years. All involving products your company distributed despite knowing they didn't meet safety standards. The fact that you avoided criminal charges doesn't mean you didn't endanger consumers."

The honey vendor was backing away. I couldn't blame her. Sure it was a great income stream to sign up with a national sales company, but you inherited their problems along with a boost to your bottom line.

Felix's hands clenched. "You almost destroyed my business with that article. We'd built relationships with dozens of small producers, we were helping them reach markets—"

"You were cutting corners on safety testing to maximize profits," Amalia said. "Don't dress up negligence as altruism."

"People make mistakes! We fixed the problems, implemented new protocols, went beyond industry standards to make sure it never happened again!" Felix's voice rose, drawing attention. "But you couldn't just report the facts—you had to write that op-ed about the hidden dangers of small-scale distribution networks and make us the poster child for everything wrong in the industry."

"If accurate reporting destroyed your business, perhaps your business was flawed."

"You don't care about accuracy. You care about making yourself look like some crusading truth-teller while you ruin people's lives." Felix stepped closer. "Do you even know what happened to my business after your article? The lawsuits from vendors who lost contracts? The employees who lost jobs? Or were you too busy accepting your journalism award?"

For the first time, I saw something flicker across Amalia's face. Not quite regret, but maybe a crack in her certainty.

"I reported the truth," she said. Her voice had lost some of its edge.

"You reported *your* version of the facts, not the truth. The one that made the best story, that fed into your reputation as the critic who isn't afraid to expose corruption." Felix's laugh was bitter. "But you know what's funny? I've rebuilt. Found new clients, implemented better systems, made the business better than before. And you? You're still doing the same thing—traveling to small towns, looking for new people to destroy. Must be exhausting, always needing fresh villains to maintain your brand."

He walked away before Amalia could respond, leaving her alone with her leather notebook held against her chest.

I expected her to make another note, to continue through the booths like nothing had happened. But instead, she stood there for a long moment. Her hand trembled.

Knox stepped back beside her, camera ready. He watched Amalia with an expression I couldn't read.

Then the moment passed. Amalia straightened her shoulders, opened her notebook to a fresh page, and continued her rounds with the same focus as before.

But I'd seen that tremor. Whatever armor Amalia wore, it wasn't as strong as she wanted people to believe.

5

The afternoon wore on, the October light beginning to slant golden across the festival, throwing long shadows. The temperature was dropping—that high-desert shift from warmth to cooling air that made you reach for the sweater you'd abandoned hours earlier.

I was helping pack up service supplies when I heard raised voices. This time, the crowd was gathering. People abandoned their booths to get a better view of whatever was happening near the main stage.

At the center, Hugo Delacroix was facing off with Amalia Limonete.

"You have absolutely no right," Hugo said. His voice carried controlled fury. "After everything you did. After what you cost me."

"I have every right," Amalia replied. Professional, cool. "It's called journalism. Perhaps if you'd been more honest about your methods from the beginning, we wouldn't be having this conversation."

"Honest?" Hugo's laugh was bitter as burnt coffee.

"You're lecturing *me* about honesty? You, who built your entire reputation by stealing other people's work?"

The crowd was growing. Vendors abandoned their booths. This was exactly the kind of spectacle that could overshadow everything good about the festival.

"I think you're confusing inspiration with theft," Amalia said. "A distinction that seems to elude many people in this industry."

"You know exactly what you did to me," Hugo said, stepping closer. "I shared my techniques, my recipes, my entire approach to fusion cuisine because I trusted you. I thought you were writing a profile, that you wanted to understand my work. Instead, you published them under your own byline in that cookbook. My grandmother's mole recipe—the one she made me promise never to share outside the family—appeared word-for-word in *Amalia's Collection* with a note about how you'd developed it during your research travels."

The crowd had gone silent. This wasn't a professional rivalry—this was personal betrayal.

"Recipe inspiration is a complex legal and ethical area—" Amalia began. "You can't copyright recipes. The entire industry shares tips and techniques."

"Don't." Hugo's voice was sharp. "Don't hide behind technicalities. You stole from me. You betrayed my trust. And now you want to write about it? Expose our professional relationship in your tell-all book? Make yourself the victim in a story where you were the one who betrayed trust?"

Another book? This was the first I'd heard about Amalia writing a tell-all book, but maybe that's why people were so confrontational.

"The public deserves to understand how this industry

really works," Amalia said. "The mentorship. The inspiration. The way techniques and recipes evolve and spread. If you're uncomfortable with transparency, perhaps you should examine your own motives."

Hugo took another step forward, close enough that I thought he might actually do something physical. But he caught himself, taking a deep breath that looked like it cost him.

"I hope your book fails," he said quietly, but his voice carried. "I hope everyone who reads it sees exactly what kind of person you are."

"Are you quite finished?" Amalia's voice was ice.

"Not even close." Hugo pulled out his phone. "Because unlike you, I document my work properly. I have emails. Photos of the handwritten recipes I shared with you. Proof of dates and conversations. And when your book comes out, if you've included anything—*anything*—that came from our time working together, I'm going to make sure everyone knows exactly where you got it."

Amalia's expression cracked—just for a second.

"You destroyed my faith in this profession," Hugo continued. "You made me question whether anything in this industry was genuine or if everyone was just looking for an angle, a way to exploit trust for personal gain. And you know what the saddest part is? You were talented once. You could have built a real career on your own work instead of stealing from everyone who was foolish enough to trust you."

He didn't wait for a response. He turned and walked away, leaving Amalia alone the target of everyone's stare and more than a few videos.

She looked around at the faces—vendors she'd critiqued, community members she'd dismissed, people whose livelihoods she'd affected. For just a moment, I saw something human in her expression. Not quite fear, but maybe the beginning of awareness that she'd made more enemies than she could handle.

Then she opened her leather notebook, made a note with hands that were steady now, and continued her booth progression like nothing had happened.

Knox had videoed the entire confrontation. When Amalia walked away, I watched Knox make another entry in his notebook.

"Well," Kashvi said when I returned to our booth, "that was illuminating."

"Illuminating and terrifying," I said. "How many other people here have that kind of history with her?"

"Want me to ask around?" Jet offered. "Discreetly?"

Before I could answer, my phone buzzed with a text from Paloma: *Get over here Now. We need to discuss tonight's tasting logistics. Some vendors getting nervous.*

Tonight. The evening tasting event that was supposed to be the festival's finale. Amalia would sample signature dishes, taking her time to evaluate each offering before announcing her impressions of Nueva Vida's culinary talents. Rajan would be there too, but she was the one every chef wanted to impress.

After watching the mounting tensions all day, after seeing how many people had old grievances with our critic, I was beginning to think that tasting might be the most charged event in Nueva Vida's history.

I walked toward the coordination tent, dodging families settling in for the evening program and vendors making final preparations. Before I arrived, I caught sight of something that made me pause.

Amalia was standing alone near the edge of the festival

grounds, her back to the crowd. Her phone was pressed to her ear, and even from a distance, I could see the rigid line of her shoulders, the way she held herself like she was bracing against wind.

"I don't care what the lawyers say," she was saying. Her voice carried in the cooling air. "The book goes forward as planned. I'm not removing the Chapter about Hugo, and I'm certainly not giving in to Octavia's threats about—"

She must have noticed someone approaching because she stopped mid-sentence, straightening her shoulders and lowering her voice.

When she turned to rejoin the festival, her professional mask was firmly in place. But I'd seen that moment of vulnerability, the exhaustion in the line of her back, the tremor in her voice when she thought no one was listening.

Whatever else Amalia Limonete was—arrogant, cruel, destructive—she was also human. Tired, pressured, maybe even scared of what she'd set in motion with her book, her reviews, her lifetime of burning bridges.

It didn't make her easier to like. But it made what was coming feel more complicated.

We still had four hours until the evening tasting. Four hours for tensions to build, old wounds to fester, and whatever was brewing between Amalia and half the festival vendors to reach its conclusion.

The weather might be perfect, but the emotional forecast looked threatening.

And somewhere in the crowd, Knox was still photographing everything. Documenting every confrontation, every moment of tension, moving through the festival. The mood made me wonder if he had a hidden motive.

6

The Nueva Vida community center didn't look like itself anymore. Fat ropes of dried red chilies hung beside string lights, casting shadows across tables draped in cream linens. The usual scent of sage and old coffee had been replaced by roasted poblanos, toasted cumin, caramelized onions, dark chocolate, and underneath it all, that earthy smell of New Mexico after rain.

Paloma gripped her clipboard with both hands, looking like she might pass out if anyone asked her a question. Near the dessert station, Knox crouched with his camera, adjusting angles to catch the chocolate displays.

Seven courses tonight. Amalia would taste signature dishes from each participating restaurant—appetizer, soup, salad, entrée, palate cleanser, second entrée, dessert. Each vendor had their prep area behind screens at the back, with servers carrying finished plates to Amalia's central table. The setup meant constant movement—vendors checking on each other, volunteers ferrying ingredients and equipment, no barriers or locked doors.

Our local business owners—people I served coffee to

every morning—were presenting their food tonight. I could see the pride and terror on their faces in equal measure.

"She's here!" Paloma materialized at my side, her voice tight. "Amalia Limonete just pulled up."

Through the open doors, I watched our guest step out of her rental car. Amalia's silver hair caught the light, and she carried herself like someone who'd never questioned her right to be anywhere.

Anthone appeared next to me, his hands shaking as he adjusted his bandana for the twentieth time.

"How do I look?" he asked.

"Like the chef you are," I said. "Confident. Professional. Ready."

His shoulders straightened a bit.

The room went quiet as Amalia entered. Every vendor, volunteer, and community member turned to watch.

She paused in the doorway, taking in the room. When she spoke, her voice carried without effort.

"Ladies and gentlemen, I appreciate the care that has gone into this evening's presentation. I'll be evaluating each offering methodically, and I ask that you allow me to focus without distraction." She moved toward her table at the center of the room. "I'll taste in the sequence presented, photographing each dish before evaluation. Please do not approach my table during the tasting process."

Don't hover, don't chatter, don't explain your food while she's eating it. Message received.

Knox was already moving through the space, his camera clicking. I watched him photograph each vendor station, chat with Felix about his cured meats, compliment Keiko on her soup presentation. He had the photographer's gift of being everywhere without being in the way.

"Knox!" Amalia called across the room, and his face

brightened. "Make sure you get the progression shots. Each course from vendor preparation through final plating."

"Already on it, Aunt Amalia." He held up his camera. "I've been documenting all week. You're going to have the most comprehensive festival coverage ever."

She smiled at him—a real smile, not the professional mask she'd been wearing. "That's my clever nephew. Your eye for composition gets better with every shoot."

The warmth between them caught me off guard. This was a different Amalia—the aunt, not the critic.

But the moment passed. Her professional expression returned as she flipped open her notebook, pulled out her gold pen, and nodded to Felix at the first station.

Felix stepped forward with his appetizer plate. I leaned forward to see how this would go.

The arrangement was beautiful—paper-thin prosciutto draped beside coins of spicy soppressata, creamy mortadella showing its fat marbling, and his grandfather's secret recipe chorizo with its paprika bloom. Shavings of aged manchego, tiny cornichons, and house-made mostarda completed the plate.

Felix explained with nervous precision. "The prosciutto is eighteen-month Spanish, the soppressata we make in-house using my grandmother's spice blend, and the mostarda features New Mexico apricots instead of traditional Italian fruit."

Amalia photographed the plate from two angles, then lifted a thin slice of prosciutto. She examined it against the light, checking the fat distribution and color, brought it to her nose, then tasted. The process took maybe thirty seconds, but it felt longer.

Her expression stayed neutral as she made notes in that shorthand I'd noticed before. Then she moved to the soppressata—same careful evaluation. Visual assessment, aroma, finally the taste. More notes.

"The fat-to-meat ratio on your soppressata is exceptional," she said, and Felix's posture changed from terrified to hopeful. "The spice blend has depth without overwhelming the pork. However," there was always a however, "your mostarda is too sweet for this application. The apricot's natural sugar content needs balancing with more acidity or heat."

Felix pulled out his notebook. "Yes. I can adjust the vinegar ratio—"

"The technique is sound," Amalia said. "This is a matter of regional adaptation. New Mexico fruit is sweeter than Italian varieties. You're on the right track."

As Felix retreated to his station, Knox photographed his relieved expression. The photographer was capturing more than just food—he was documenting the whole emotional arc.

Behind the prep screens, vendors moved between their areas. Keiko checked something simmering on a portable burner, while Hugo arranged micro-greens with tweezers. Anthone touched each ingredient to verify it was where he needed it.

The soup course arrived. A server set a wide, shallow bowl before Amalia. Keiko's poblano corn chowder looked like liquid gold—creamy and rich, with crema creating swirls on the surface. Toasted pepitas and fresh cilantro added texture and color. The aroma reached me from across the room—smoky roasted poblanos, sweet corn, chicken stock, a whisper of cumin.

Knox was there with his camera. "The color gradient is gorgeous, Keiko," he said. "Can I get a shot of your prep station? Show people the behind-the-scenes work?"

"Of course." Keiko's voice shook a bit. "The poblanos are back there cooling. I just finished charring them."

He disappeared behind the screens while Amalia began her evaluation. She photographed the soup from two angles, then leaned forward to inhale the steam. Her eyes closed briefly—the first time I'd seen her drop her guard during tasting.

The first spoonful took forever. She held it in her mouth, analyzing the layers, the way heat built from the poblanos. I held my breath. From the nervous shuffling around the room, I wasn't alone.

"Impressive," Amalia said, and I heard Keiko exhale. "The poblanos are perfectly charred—smoky without bitterness. The corn provides natural sweetness that balances the capsaicin heat. Your roux technique is flawless; this has body without heaviness."

She took another spoonful. "The pepitas add necessary texture." More notes in that leather journal. "This is comfort food executed at a technical level that respects both tradition and innovation."

Knox emerged from behind the screens. He caught my eye and grinned. "This is incredible material. Aunt Amalia's going to love these."

The salad course came from Hugo's station. After tasting, Amelia made a note in her book. "The composition is striking," she said, lifting her fork. "Technically precise knife work on the radishes. The candied pecans show proper caramelization—no crystallization, good snap."

Knox moved toward the salad area. "Hugo, mind if I grab some shots of your ingredient prep? Those candied pecans look great."

"Fine." Hugo stepped aside to let Knox in. I watched the

photographer document the organization, the professional equipment, the precision of Hugo's setup.

Anthone's entrée came next, and my heart rate picked up. The server carried forward his Southwest fusion creation on a charcoal-gray dish—seared ahi tuna with a green chili crust, positioned atop forbidden black rice, surrounded by a ginger-soy reduction dotted with sriracha oil, finished with pickled jalapeño slices and micro cilantro.

The presentation was magazine-worthy. The tuna showed perfect sear marks, the green crust visible as a delicate coating. The black rice provided texture and visual drama. The sauce work was precise—reduction and sriracha creating swooshes and dots.

Amalia photographed from four angles, taking her time. "Ambitious," she said. She cut into the tuna, revealing the rare center—pink, still cool. The green chili crust held together.

The first bite involved all components—tuna, rice, sauce, a single pickled jalapeño. I watched her face, looking for any hint.

She chewed slowly, analyzing. The wait felt eternal.

"This is sophisticated fusion executed at a high level," she said, and I saw Anthone's hands clench. "The tuna is precisely cooked—rare center, proper sear. The green chili crust adds complexity without competing with the fish's delicate flavor. The pairing with Asian elements is unexpected but successful."

More notes, her gold pen moving across the page.

"The forbidden rice provides earthy undertones that ground the dish. Your sauce work shows technical understanding—the reduction has proper consistency, and the sriracha dots are measured to provide heat accents rather than overwhelming spice." She took another sample, just tuna and crust. "The pickling liquid on the jalapeños is well-balanced. They provide acid and heat without dominating."

She looked up at where Anthone stood frozen. "This demonstrates genuine creativity and solid technical foundation. You have a sophisticated palate and the skills to execute your vision."

I heard Kashvi's soft squeal of excitement, quickly muffled. Anthone looked like he might cry.

Knox headed toward the fusion station. "Anthone, I need to get shots of your plating technique. That sauce work is incredible. How do you get the dots so uniform?"

As Anthone explained his squeeze bottle method, I noticed Amalia had moved on to her palate cleanser—a simple lime sorbet in a small glass bowl. She gave it the same attention she'd given everything else. Two photographs, visual assessment of the texture, then careful tasting.

"Properly executed," she said. "Clean lime flavor, good acid balance, smooth texture without ice crystals. Appropriate portion size for palate refreshment between courses."

The second entrée received the same warm treatment. Two visiting chefs who'd set up booths for just this experience.

With so little drama in the tasting, my attention had been drawn to the way people moved through the event. Vendors drifted freely between their prep areas and the main room, checking on colleagues, gathering ingredients from shared supplies in the back. Servers carried plates and retrieved empty dishes. Knox wandered everywhere with his camera, welcomed at every station. Even the volunteers had access to all areas.

It was a warm, collaborative atmosphere—exactly what you'd want from a community celebration. It left me wondering what had changed with Amalia. She was never this supportive, or gentle with her 'howevers'. Tonight the errors were treated gently and with encouragement.

Rajan had positioned himself near the appetizer station to observe Amalia's technique, but I'd noticed him venture into several prep areas. Hugo had left his station multiple times to consult with servers about timing. Keiko had helped with something at the dessert area. Even Knox, with his friendly photographer's access, had been behind every single prep screen at least once.

The first dessert course arrived—all vendors produced a sweet ending for judgment.

Chocolate mousse, Alistair's contribution. Old-fashioned, like his cafe. He presented it in individual glass cups, each one a work of art. Dark chocolate mousse so rich it was almost black, topped with a quenelle of whipped cream, finished with a chocolate curl and a single fresh raspberry. Someone on his staff clearly knew about food art.

Knox appeared beside her table. "This is the money shot."

"Then you'd better capture it before I destroy the composition," Amalia replied. She waited while Knox took several photographs.

When he stepped back, she lifted her spoon and took a small taste of just the mousse—no cream, no garnish.

Her eyes closed. Not a brief flutter, but a genuine moment of appreciation.

"This," she said quietly, "is exceptional."

The room went silent.

"The chocolate quality is superior—I taste single-origin cocoa, probably Ecuadorian given the floral notes. The texture is perfect; you've achieved proper aeration without sacrificing density. There's a whisper of espresso enhancing the chocolate without making itself known as a separate flavor. The vanilla is real, not extract, and measured precisely."

This time adding the cream to the spoon, she tasted again. "The cream provides necessary contrast—sweetness and lightness against the mousse's intensity. The raspberry adds acid that cuts through the richness at exactly the right moment." More notes. "This is comfort food elevated to fine dining execution. Forty years of technique showing in every element."

I thought Alistair would faint.

7

"She looks happy," Kashvi said, nodding toward where Amalia surveyed her next dessert plate. "When's the last time someone served her six perfect desserts in one sitting?"

"Never, probably." I watched Amalia held the plate up for pictures before taking her first bite. Even her happy face was intimidating. "Most restaurants can barely manage one dish she can't tear apart."

Then she moved to Keiko's bread pudding. I held my breath. The poor girl had been through enough with Amalia. Would this course undermine the positive of the soup?

She took a forkful, closing her eyes as she chewed. Her expression stayed neutral. Then something shifted. Her eyebrows drew together, not in disappointment but confusion, like she'd tasted something unexpected.

Amalia reached for her water glass. Her hand trembled as she brought it to her lips, but she didn't drink. She pressed her other hand to her chest, fingers splayed across her sternum. The confusion on her face deepened into fear.

"Is she choking?" someone asked from a nearby table.

But it wasn't choking. I'd worked in enough kitchens to recognize distress, and this was different. Amalia's breathing had gone rapid and shallow, her skin flushing.

I rushed in to help and caught a faint but unmistakable scent of bitter almonds. Not the sweet, marzipan scent of almond extract, but something sharper. Chemical.

My blood went cold.

"Kashvi, call 911," I said. "Tell them I think she'd been poisoned."

The sound of Amalia's breathing cut through the murmur of conversation, harsh and labored. She tried to stand, gripping the edge of the table, but her legs wouldn't support her. Knox was there, catching her before she hit the floor.

"Aunt Amalia?" Knox's voice cracked. "What's wrong? Someone help her!"

Amalia went limp in Knox's arms, her breathing coming in short, desperate gasps. The bitter almond scent was stronger here, and I saw the signs I'd only read about in culinary safety courses—the flush spreading across her face and neck, her dilated pupils, the confused, vacant look in her eyes.

"Lay her down," I told Knox, keeping my voice steady even as my heart hammered. "On her side."

Knox lowered his aunt to the floor with surprising gentleness, his hands shaking. "What's happening to her? Is it an allergic reaction?"

"Everyone give her space!" George's voice cut through the panic as he pushed through the crowd. Thank God for that security arrangement. Without an official role, I didn't think he'd be in attendance. "Has someone called for an ambulance?"

"On the way," Jet confirmed, phone still pressed to his ear.

"It's not an allergic reaction," I told George as he knelt beside Amalia. "I smell bitter almonds. This is cyanide poisoning."

George's expression went from concerned to grim. He checked Amalia's pulse, his jaw tightening. "How certain are you?"

"The scent, the symptoms, the speed—" I gestured to Amalia's flushed face, her labored breathing despite the seizure subsiding. "It all fits."

"Yes,this is a crime scene." George looked up at the uniformed officers who'd appeared at the edges of the crowd. "Nobody touches anything on that dessert table. I want samples of every dish preserved as they are."

Detective Denise Collett appeared beside him, her eyes scanning the scene. "What do we have?"

"Suspected poisoning," George reported. "Cyanide, based on presentation. Victim consumed multiple dishes before collapse."

Amalia's breathing grew more erratic, each gasp more desperate. Knox had sunk to his knees beside her, one hand gripping hers, his face pale.

"Aunt Amalia, please," he whispered. "Please hold on."

But I could see it in George's face, in the way Detective Collett's expression shifted from alert to resigned. Cyanide worked fast. By the time symptoms showed, it was often too late.

The EMTs arrived, their equipment clattering as they took over from George. They worked fast, checking vitals, starting an IV, preparing to move Amalia. But even as they lifted her onto the stretcher, I could see the truth in their body language—they were going through the motions because it was what they were trained to do, not because they expected it to make a difference.

"I'm coming with her," Knox said, moving to follow the stretcher.

"Sir, we need to ask you some questions—" Detective Collett began.

"She's my aunt!" Knox's voice cracked. "I'm not letting her go alone!"

George exchanged a glance with Detective Collett, then nodded. "Go. But we'll need to speak with you soon."

The EMTs wheeled Amalia toward the door, Knox trailing behind them like a man in a nightmare. The last thing I saw before they disappeared was his hand reaching for his aunt's, fingers intertwining with hers.

"All right, everyone, I need your attention." George's voice carried the authority of his position. "This is now a crime scene. No one leaves until we've taken your contact information and initial statement."

A murmur of fear rippled through the crowd.

"Was it really poison?" Keiko's voice wavered from near the kitchen. She looked like she might be sick. "Someone poisoned her?"

"We don't know anything for certain yet," Detective Collett said, though her tone suggested otherwise. "But we're treating this as a suspicious incident. That means we need to preserve all evidence and interview everyone who could get into the food preparation area."

Paloma, who'd been standing frozen near the head table, shook off her shock. "Dear God. The festival. This is going to destroy us."

"Ms. Santos, I understand your concern," George said. "But right now, we have a possible homicide to investigate."

"Possible?" Anthone had moved to stand beside me, his face ashen. "Eliza said it was cyanide."

"I said suspected cyanide," I corrected quietly. "Based on symptoms."

"How long does cyanide take to work?" Kashvi asked.

"Minutes," I said. "Sometimes less, depending on the dose."

Whoever had done this had been in this room, had watched Amalia eat, had known what they were doing.

George approached the dessert table, Detective Collett beside him. They moved carefully, documenting everything with their phones before touching anything. Six perfect desserts, each one a potential murder weapon.

"We'll need to know who prepared each dish," Detective Collett said, making notes. "And who had access to them before they were served."

Vic helped me into a chair. "That's going to be a long list," he said. "She wasn't exactly known for making friends."

"Then we'd better get started." Detective Collett surveyed the crowd. I recognized her expression, she was calculating how many interviews she'd be conducting tonight. "I want everyone who prepared food separated from the general attendees. George, will you handle scene documentation?"

"Already on it." George was using his phone to photographing the table from every angle, careful not to disturb anything. "I'll get samples of every dish to the lab tonight."

I watched him work, my mind trying to process what had happened. One minute, Amalia had been enjoying dessert. The next, she'd been fighting for her life while fifty witnesses watched. If I was right, the poison was in the dessert. I was glad she hadn't tasted all of them. Then I realized I was making a bad assumption. The poisoner could be anyone, not just the chef who prepared each one.

"Eliza." Vic touched my arm. "You okay?"

"I don't know," I admitted. "I've seen a lot since moving to Nueva Vida, but watching someone die right in front of me—" I stopped.

"She's not dead yet," Kashvi said, though her voice lacked conviction. "Maybe the EMTs can save her."

We all knew better. Cyanide didn't give second chances.

"Everyone who prepared desserts tonight, please move to the left side of the room," Detective Collett called out. "Everyone else, remain where you are. We'll be taking your statements shortly."

Anthone moved toward the designated area, joining Keiko, Alistair, and the other dessert vendors. They clustered together, which I supposed they were.

"This can't be happening," I heard Alistair mutter. "I've been cooking for thirty years. I've never poisoned anyone."

"None of us have," Keiko said, but her voice shook. "But someone did. Someone in this room put cyanide in that food."

The fear was palpable now. Vendors who'd been friends this morning now eyed each other with suspicion. Community leaders who'd celebrated Nueva Vida's culinary talent now looked like they'd rather be anywhere else.

George's phone lit up. He stepped away to answer it, his expression growing grimmer. When he ended the call, he exchanged a long look with Detective Collett before turning to address the room.

"I've just received word from the hospital," he said. "Amalia Limonete was pronounced dead fifteen minutes ago. This is now a homicide investigation."

Dead. The woman who'd terrified restaurant owners

across the Southwest, who'd built a career on perfect taste and merciless criticism, was gone.

"Oh my God," someone whispered.

"This can't be real," another voice said.

But it was real. The festival that was supposed to put Nueva Vida on the culinary map had just become the site of a murder that would make national news for all the wrong reasons.

Cleo Fontaine, Amalia's assistant, pushed through the crowd, her face streaked with tears. "Where is she? I need to see her!"

"Your name?" Detective Collett asked.

"Cleo. She was my boss. She can't be dead." Cleo's voice broke. "She can't be. We had so much work to do, so many stories to finish—" She stopped. "Her notebook. Where's her notebook?"

Everyone's attention shifted.

"What notebook?" Detective Collett asked.

"The leather one she always carried. It had all her notes, her research, everything she was working on." Cleo looked around. "It was right beside her plate. I saw it when the desserts were served."

George and Detective Collett moved back to the dessert table. They searched the area, then widened to include the floor and nearby chairs.

Nothing.

"When did you last see it?" George asked.

"Right before she started eating," Cleo said. "She'd made a note about the bread pudding's presentation. That notebook went everywhere with her—she'd never leave it behind."

"Maybe it's with her personal effects at the hospital," someone suggested.

Not likely—the EMTs moved fast. In the chaos of the medical emergency, someone had been cool-headed enough to steal what might be the most incriminating evidence in the room.

"So we're looking for someone who not only poisoned Amalia Limonete," Detective Collett said, "but who also managed to take that notebook when everyone was watching the EMTs."

"What was in the notebook?" I asked Cleo. "Besides her review notes?"

Cleo wiped her eyes, trying to compose herself. "Everything. She was working on multiple stories—exposés about the food industry, investigative pieces about restaurant fraud, profiles of chefs with interesting back stories. That notebook was her entire professional life."

"And now it's evidence in her murder," George said. "Which means whoever took it either wanted to hide what she'd written about them, or wanted to make sure we couldn't see what she'd discovered."

Detective Collett began organizing officers to take statements. The festival attendees were separated into groups—chefs who'd prepared the desserts—the most probably murder weapon. Other vendors, community leaders, and general guests. Each group would be interviewed separately, their movements tracked, their alibis verified.

Vic and I stayed where we were. If no one pushed us into a suspect group, neither of us was volunteering. I needed to stay free to help Anthone.

Knox returned while they were organizing, his face pale and streaked with tears. He moved through the crowd unseeing until he reached the spot where his aunt had fallen.

"She's gone," he said to no one in particular. "Just like

that. One minute she was eating dessert, the next—" His voice broke.

Vic moved to intercept him before he could contaminate the crime scene. "Mr. Thorne, I'm so sorry for your loss. But the police need to preserve this area for the investigation."

Knox looked at him with red-rimmed eyes. "Investigation. Right. Because someone murdered her." He laughed without humor. "God knows she made enough enemies. But to do it here, in front of everyone—"

"When did you last speak with your aunt?" Detective Collett asked gently.

"This afternoon. She was excited about the festival, about the quality of the food. Said it was the best small-town culinary event she'd attended in years." Knox's hands clenched. "She was happy. When's the last time Amalia Limonete was happy about anything?"

"Did she mention anyone she was concerned about?" George asked. "Anyone who'd threatened her, or who she planned to write negatively about?"

Knox's laugh was hollow. "She wrote bad stuff about everyone. That was her job. But actually threatening her? No one was ever stupid enough to do that to her face."

But someone had been desperate enough to use poison.

"Mr. Thorne, we're going to need a formal statement," Detective Collett said. "And we'll need to know about anyone who might have wanted to harm your aunt."

"It might not help," Knox said. "Amalia didn't believe in making friends. She believed in telling the truth, no matter who it hurt." He looked around at the assembled vendors and guests. "Any one of these people could have had a reason. Hell, half the restaurants in America wanted her dead."

"But only one of them did it," George said.

Someone in this room—someone I'd smiled at, maybe talked to—had committed murder. They'd looked Amalia in the eye, served her poisoned food, and watched her die.

"You should sit down," Vic said, guiding me toward a chair. "You look pale."

I sat, grateful for his steady presence.

Across the room, Anthone caught my eye. He looked terrified. His mango cake had been on that plate, not eaten, but what if the killer poisoned every dessert? He'd be near the top of the suspect list, along with every other vendor who'd prepared tonight's sweet course. On top of that list were Keiko and Alistair. The two dishes she'd sampled.

George approached us. "Eliza, I'm going to need you to walk me through everything you saw tonight. Starting from when the desserts were plated."

"Of course." I stood, trying to organize my thoughts. "George, I recognized the symptoms because of my cooking background. Bitter almonds, rapid breathing, the flush—"

"I know," he said. "And that knowledge is going to be noted in your statement. I can't give you special treatment on this one. Too many people saw you near the victim, and your team prepared one of the meals she consumed."

I understood. The amateur sleuth who'd helped solve previous cases had just become a potential suspect.

Detective Collett coordinated with the officers, establishing a perimeter around the serving table. The desserts themselves sat there like exhibits in a museum of murder—beautiful, deadly, untouchable.

"I want every dish logged and photographed before we move it," she instructed. "And I need samples of everything sent to the lab tonight. I don't care if we have to wake up the toxicologists—this takes priority."

What had happened was starting to sink in for everyone.

The excited chatter of earlier had been replaced by hushed whispers and fearful glances. Vendors who'd been friendly this morning now stood apart, each one wondering if the person next to them was a killer.

Texts started coming in—from Alf, from Martha, Brad, Vic's uncle, from neighbors I'd served coffee to this morning. Word was spreading through Nueva Vida, and by tomorrow, the whole world would know what had happened here.

George's phone rang. He moved to the side to answer it. I couldn't see his expression, but his body tensed so it wasn't good news. When he returned, he gathered Detective Collett and the other officers for a brief huddle.

"What now?" I asked Vic quietly.

"I don't know, but it doesn't look good."

George broke away from the huddle and addressed the room. "I've just been informed that we're going to have to keep everyone here longer than anticipated. The State Police are sending investigators, and they'll want to interview everyone while the scene is fresh."

People groaned. It was past midnight. Some had been here since early afternoon.

"I understand this is inconvenient," George continued. "But someone in this room committed murder tonight. We need to find out who before they have a chance to destroy more evidence or flee."

The word "flee" sent unease through the crowd. Someone looked toward the exits, where uniformed officers now stood.

"No one is being detained," Detective Collett clarified. "But we do need everyone's cooperation. The faster we can take statements and collect evidence, the faster everyone can go home."

Kashvi stood beside me, Jet close behind. My found family, rallying in crisis like we always did.

"This is bad," Kashvi whispered. "How is George going to deal with the State Police taking over?"

"I don't know. How are we going to get information if he's cut out?" I glanced over at George. "This is really bad."

But it was about to get worse.

George's phone pinged. This time, when he read the message, his face went still. He showed the screen to Detective Collett, who cursed under her breath.

"What?" I couldn't help asking.

George looked at me, and for a moment, his professional mask slipped. "The preliminary field test came back on the desserts. They all tested negative for cyanide."

If the desserts weren't poisoned, then the cyanide had been delivered some other way. The list of suspects had just expanded from the dessert vendors to everyone in the room.

"How is that possible?" Anthone asked. "If she was poisoned with cyanide, it had to be in something she ate or drank."

"Not necessarily," Detective Collett said. "Cyanide can be absorbed through skin contact in some forms. Or it could have been in something she consumed before the desserts —something we haven't considered yet."

She was right. Amalia had eaten an entire multi-course meal tonight. Any one of those dishes could have been the delivery method. Or it could have been her water glass, her wine, even the fork she'd eaten with.

8

I gave up on sleep around four and arrived at EB Eats by five-thirty, beating the sunrise. Macchiato had spent most of the night on my chest, but her purring hadn't helped. Every time I closed my eyes, I saw Amalia's face—shock, then nothing.

The diner was quiet in a way that felt wrong. I started the coffee, fired up the grill, pulled ingredients for prep. My hands shook through all of it.

Anthone showed up at six without his usual energy. "How'd you sleep?"

"Didn't." I cracked eggs into a bowl. "You?"

"Same." He pulled ingredients for the day's specials, but his mind was elsewhere. "Festival's canceled. Paloma called me at midnight, crying. She thinks Nueva Vida's reputation is shot."

I thought about that—one night undoing years of work. The Charity Food Fair was always a success. Now we'd be the town where a critic got murdered.

"Did George or Detective Collett call you?" I asked.

"This morning at five." Anthone's jaw tightened. "They

want me at the station at nine for an interview. I told them I'd be there in the afternoon. I can't leave you without help."

The diner door opened. I looked up expecting an early regular and got George with Detective Denise Collett instead, both carrying folders thick enough to suggest they'd been working all night.

"Morning, Eliza." George's voice was professional but not cold. "We have some follow-up questions. Got a few minutes?"

I glanced at the empty dining room. "Sure. Coffee?"

"Please." He slid into a booth. Collett took the seat across from him. I poured three cups and brought them over with cream and sugar.

"We've been conducting interviews since last night," George said, pulling out a notepad covered in his neat handwriting. "Timeline reconstruction, evidence collection, the usual. Lab's processing the food samples now—should have preliminary results by noon."

"Cyanide?" I asked, hoping for some confirmation of the method as I sat with my own coffee.

"We're working on that assumption," Collett said, her tone neutral. "But we need lab confirmation before we can narrow down the delivery method."

"What about the state police?" I asked. I'd kind of thought George and Detective Collett would be sidelined. Maybe too many TV shows.

"Got delayed." George flipped through his notes. "We've interviewed Hugo Delacroix, Rajan Okoye, Octavia Beaumont, and Felix Kowalski so far. All have weak alibis for the critical window between when Amalia's dessert was plated and when she consumed it."

"Weak how?" I asked.

"I'm sure the rumor mill will have this anyway. They

were all moving around the festival area," Collett said. "Multiple witnesses place each of them near the tasting pavilion at various times, but no one can account for their exact movements during the fifteen-minute window when the poison was most likely introduced."

I thought about that timeline. "So anyone could have tampered with her dessert?"

"In theory." George took a sip of coffee. "But unless the preliminary tests were faulty, it wasn't the desserts. Anyway, the setup makes it tricky. The desserts were plated by individual vendors at their booths, then carried to the tasting pavilion by festival volunteers. Amalia's assistant, Cleo Fontaine, was supervising the sequence. Anyone could have added something to just part of a dish."

"I met Cleo briefly," I said. "She seemed devastated."

"She is." George's expression softened. "We interviewed her first thing this morning. She's being cooperative, but she's also grief-stricken. Apparently she'd worked with Amalia for three years."

"That's why we want to ask you about something," Collett said, her sharp gaze on me. "Several witnesses mentioned that you were coordinating between vendors and the tasting pavilion. What exactly did that involve?"

I walked them through my role—making sure the courses came out in the right order, checking with each vendor before their dish was served, troubleshooting any last-minute issues. It felt mundane when I described it, but George made notes.

"Did you notice anyone behaving strangely?" he asked. "Anyone who seemed nervous or who was paying unusual attention to Amalia's food?"

I thought back, trying to separate normal festival stress from something more sinister. "Everyone was nervous. This was a major event for Nueva Vida, and Amalia's reputation made people extra careful. But..." I paused, remembering. "Hugo seemed more agitated than nervous. And Octavia kept trying to corner Amalia between courses."

"We already know about those details," George said. "Hugo and Amalia have a complicated history. And Octavia's been trying to get Amalia on her show for months."

"Complicated enough to kill over?" I asked. "Hugo, I mean."

Collett's expression stayed neutral. "We're not ruling anyone out at this stage. But we're also not jumping to conclusions. Good police work means following the evidence, not our assumptions."

The door opened again. Kashvi rushed in, saw George and Collett, and stopped. "Oh. Sorry. I didn't mean to interrupt."

"It's fine," George said, standing. "We're finished here for now. Eliza, if you remember anything else, call me. Anything—even if it seems small."

After they left, Kashvi slid into the booth George had vacated. "So?"

"So they're conducting a professional investigation," I said. "Keeping details away from nosy diner owners. They're good at their jobs, Kashvi."

"But?"

"The state police didn't show. I know our two detectives are capable, but I wonder if they know enough about our industry." I topped off both our coffees. "They might be asking the right questions, but they're asking them to the wrong people. Or in the wrong way."

"We know that. People have gotten over the fact they are

both incomers," Kashvi said, "but, community information doesn't always flow through official channels."

"Is that what we're calling gossip now?" I thought about all the small-town dynamics that George and Detective Collett would never hear about because secrets needed to be protected. "They're focused on evidence and timeline. We can focus on motive and relationships."

"The EB Eats Investigation Society rides again?" Kashvi asked with a slight smile.

"Maybe." I glanced toward the kitchen, where Anthone was prepping despite his upcoming police interview. Jacquie would be in soon to take over the kitchen, Will and Lola the serving. We'd both be free to help with the investigation in our own ways. "But we need to be smart about it. George has valid concerns about us interfering again."

"So we don't interfere," Kashvi said. "We supplement. We talk to people who won't talk to cops. We use our connections to understand context. Then we share what we learn."

It made sense in theory. In practice, I knew it would be more complicated. But sitting around doing nothing while Nueva Vida's reputation crumbled wasn't an option either.

By mid-morning, word had spread through town about the festival cancellation. The usual breakfast rush at EB Eats was replaced by a steady stream of worried locals, all asking the same questions: *Was it really murder? Are we safe? What's going to happen to Nueva Vida?*

Martha Hendricks, who ran the post office and lately the historical society sat in her usual booth. She knew everyone's business and helped us on previous investigations. "Not the food," she corrected a neighbor. "They don't know how it was done, but someone poisoned that poor woman."

"Martha, you don't know that," Will said, refilling her coffee. But the damage was done. Within an hour, half the town would be convinced they knew exactly how Amalia died, even if the details were pure speculation.

I was wiping down the counter when the door opened and Paloma walked in. Her eyes showed the effects of a long crying session.

"Paloma, sit down." I motioned to the free stool at the counter. "What can I get you?"

"Coffee, please. And maybe five minutes of your time?" She slid onto the seat and put her elbows on the counter.

I poured her coffee and pushed the cream and sugar closer. "I'm so sorry about what happened."

"Everyone keeps saying that." Paloma wrapped both hands around the mug. "But sorry doesn't change the fact that someone died at my event. Sorry doesn't fix Nueva Vida's reputation or bring back the tourism dollars we were counting on."

I wasn't all that sure tourists would stay away, but they were important to my bottom line too. "How bad is it?"

"Three vendors have already called to cancel their bookings for the farmer's market. The hotel's had two group cancellations. And the mayor's office is fielding calls from concerned businesses." She took a shaky sip of coffee. "Nueva Vida's food scene was getting recognition, and now we're going to be known as the place where a famous food critic was murdered."

"The police will solve this," I said, with more confidence than I felt. "Maybe we'll attract the murder junkie crowd." My attempt at humor didn't land quite as well as I hoped.

"Will they?" Paloma's eyes met mine. "Detective Kramer might not be allowed to investigate when the state police arrive."

I thought about that—the small businesses that depended on tourist dollars, the families who'd invested everything in making Nueva Vida a destination. One unsolved murder could destroy years of work.

"There's something else," Paloma said. "I've been organizing events here for twenty years. I know when something's off. And yesterday, before the tasting started, I saw things."

"What kind of things?"

"Arguments. Tension. Hugo Delacroix and Amalia had words near the dessert station. Octavia Beaumont was practically stalking her between courses. And Felix Kowalski—he kept watching her with this look on his face. Not anger exactly, but something close to it."

"Did you tell the police?"

"I gave a statement last night." She set down her coffee cup. "But I told them facts. Timeline, logistics, who was where. I didn't tell them about the undercurrents, the history, the way people's faces changed when Amalia walked by."

"Why not?"

Paloma met my eyes. "Because facts are easy. Context is hard. And I'm not sure they'd listen."

She left twenty minutes later, after finishing her coffee. Some of what she'd told me was useful—specific times, movements, overheard conversations. Some was just anxiety from someone whose life's work had been destroyed in one night.

But she'd reminded me that this murder affected more than just Amalia and whoever killed her. It affected everyone who'd worked to build something worth protecting.

At noon, Jet showed up at the diner. "Kashvi called. She wants to meet at The Open Page in an hour."

"Investigation strategy session?" I asked.

"Something like that." He glanced around the dining room, which had emptied out after the lunch rush. "Are we really doing this again?"

"Do we have a choice?" I pulled off my apron and called back to the kitchen. "Jacquie, I'm taking a break. You good?"

"Go." She appeared in the pass-through window. "But be careful. George isn't going to be happy if you start interfering."

"We're not interfering," I said. "We're supplementing."

Jet raised an eyebrow but didn't comment.

The Open Page was quiet when we arrived. Kashvi had the back room set up with coffee, snacks. We'd moved our murder board back to her place after Macchiato showed her displeasure by tangling up the red string and chewing through half the sticky notes.

"Okay," Kashvi said, once we were all settled. "George and Denise are conducting a professional investigation. They're doing everything by the book—interviews, evidence collection, lab analysis. They're good at what they do."

"But?" Jet prompted.

"Not so much a but," I said. "They need our help, just like the last cases. I'm not saying they wouldn't have solved them, but it would have taken way longer without us. We need this solved fast so we don't get labeled the murder capital of New Mexico."

Slipped in to join us. "Interview is done. They asked about food prep, timeline. All the technical stuff. But they didn't ask about relationships or history or why anyone would want Amalia dead. I'd think motive would be super important."

"Maybe there are too many people with motive," Kashvi said. "I doesn't matter. We can work backward—start with motive and relationships, then look for evidence that fits."

I wasn't sure that would pan out, but we needed some kind of plan.

"So what's your suggestion?" Jet asked.

Kashvi didn't answer him. She looked at me and held up a marker ready to add things to the board.

I thought about Paloma's words, about Martha's gossip, about the gossip that never made it into official police reports. "We use our community connections. We ask questions that focus on why, not just what and when. We follow up on rumors."

"And we share everything we learn with George," Kashvi added. "We're not trying to solve this ourselves. We're trying to give them context they wouldn't have otherwise."

"Community intelligence gathering," Jet said. "Or as we usually call it, gossip. I can use my tour guide network. People talk to me because I'm not official—I'm just Jet who shows them around town."

"Food industry insider knowledge," Anthone offered. "I can analyze how someone could have introduced poison without being detected. Even if it's not in the food. When they would have had access, what ingredients were available, how the dessert courses were handled."

"And I'll coordinate," I said. "Talk to festival vendors, business owners, anyone who interacted with Amalia. Map who's connected to who and what tensions are under the surface."

We spent the next hour dividing responsibilities and setting ground rules. No confronting suspects. No withholding information from the police. No taking unnecessary risks. This wasn't about playing detective—it was about protecting our community and helping George do his job.

As we were wrapping up, my phone pinged. A text from George: *Need to speak with you. Can you come by the station?*

"That was fast," Jet said, reading over my shoulder.

"Small town," Kashvi said. "He probably heard we were meeting."

I grabbed my purse and headed for the door. "Let's hope he understands what we're trying to do."

9

George was waiting in an interview room, not his office. More formal, more official. Detective Collett was there too.

"Sit," George said, his tone neutral.

I sat.

"I heard you've been talking to Paloma Santos," he began. "And that you're planning to conduct some kind of informal investigation with your friends."

"We're gathering community information," I said. "Talking to people who might not be comfortable giving statements to police. We're not interfering with your investigation."

"That's a fine line, Eliza." George leaned back in his chair. "And it's one you've walked before. Successfully, I'll admit. But this case is different."

Why didn't he give me credit? I mean, no one had been hurt when we did this before. Yes, came close, but not actually hurt. "Different how?"

Collett spoke up. "We have reason to believe Amalia

wasn't just here to review restaurants. She was investigating someone. We don't know who or why. Or, even if it was true."

"Hugo accused her of staling his recipes. Maybe it was the other way around. She came here to avoid someone?" I thought about Cleo's vague comments about Amalia's research.

"That's our working theory," George said. "Which means we're not just dealing with a crime of passion or a restaurant rivalry. We're dealing with someone who was desperate enough to commit premeditated murder. One that took planning."

"And you think that person would be dangerous to us," I said.

"I think that person has already killed once to protect their secrets," George said. "And I think anyone who gets too close to discovering those same secrets could be at risk."

I met his eyes. "So, are you saying we shouldn't help?"

"I want you to be careful," George said. "I want you to understand that this isn't a game. And I want you to promise that if you learn anything significant, you'll bring it to us immediately. Not after you've investigated further, not after you've talked to more people—immediately."

"We can do that," I said. Well, it would depend on the circumstances, right?

"I mean it, Eliza." George looked me in the eye. "I care about what happens to you. All of you. And I can't do my job if I'm constantly worried about you putting yourself in danger."

"We'll be careful. I promise." There was that protective streak again.

Collett stood. "One more thing. We're interviewing Cleo Fontaine again this afternoon. She's staying at the Desert

Rose Inn if you want to talk to her. Might be good for her to talk to someone who isn't law enforcement."

Permission to use our community connections, as long as we shared what we learned. I'd take it.

"Thank you," I said. "For trusting us."

"I'm trusting you," George corrected. "Don't make me regret it."

THE DESERT ROSE Inn was Nueva Vida's nicest hotel, which wasn't saying much. Clean rooms, decent Wi-Fi, acceptable breakfast bar. I found Cleo in the small lobby, curled up in an armchair with a cold cup of tea and red-rimmed eyes.

"Cleo?" I said. "I'm Eliza Burton. We met briefly yesterday at the festival."

She looked up, recognition on her face. "The diner owner. You were helping coordinate everything."

"I was. I'm so sorry about Amalia."

Cleo's face crumpled. For a moment I thought she might start crying again. But she pulled herself together. "Everyone keeps saying that. But it doesn't change anything."

I sat down in the chair across from her. "Would you like to talk? Sometimes it's harder when you're alone. Nothing official. Just... talk."

She studied me for a moment, then nodded. "I could use some coffee. Real coffee, not whatever this is." She gestured at the cold tea.

We walked to EB Eats, making small talk about the weather and the desert landscape. Jacquie took one look at Cleo's face and started making food without being asked—grilled cheese and tomato soup, comfort food.

Once we had coffee and were sitting in a booth, Cleo

spoke. "She wasn't supposed to die here. We were supposed to finish the festival reviews, drive to Santa Fe, work on her article. She had a deadline next week."

"What kind of article?" I asked, though I suspected I knew.

Cleo surveyed the dining room, checking who might overhear. "She was investigating something about the industry. I'm not sure what exactly, but she said it would be big."

"Did she tell you who she suspected?"

"She was paranoid about leaks," Cleo said. "Everything important was in her leather notebook, written in shorthand only she could read quickly. But I overheard phone calls, saw meeting notes. Several people at the festival were going to be named in her article."

How bad could it be? "So this wasn't about a bad review. It was about exposure for something much more serious than a nasty review."

"Exactly." Cleo's hands tightened around her coffee mug. "And yesterday morning, someone called and threatened her. Told her to leave town immediately or face consequences."

"Did she report it?"

"She laughed it off. Said she'd been getting threats for years, that it came with the territory." Cleo's voice broke slightly. "I should have insisted she take it seriously."

Will slid her food on the table. "Eat up. The best cooking in the state."

I smiled at his attempt to promote us. "This isn't your fault," I said to Cleo. "But it does help us understand what we're dealing with."

We talked for another hour. Cleo shared details about Amalia's research methods, her targets, the kind of evidence she'd been gathering. She also mentioned something George had asked about—that Amalia was very open about her sensitivity to bitter flavors, a professional habit she'd developed over years of food criticism.

"Anyone who'd worked with food critics before would know," Cleo said. "It's standard practice to disclose taste sensitivities during festivals. Helps vendors adjust their presentations. No wants to lose points for something as silly as preferences."

Which meant the killer had access to information that would help them mask the cyanide's bitter almond taste. Chocolate would be perfect—rich enough to hide the poison, familiar enough not to raise suspicion.

When Cleo left to go back to her hotel, I sat at the counter and made notes. Facts, not speculation. Timeline details and overheard conversations. Context that George would need.

Jacquie emerged from the kitchen with two bowls of green chili stew. "You look like you need this."

"I need a lot of things," I said. "But food's a good start."

She joined me at the counter and we ate in silence for a few minutes before she said, "So you're really doing this? Taking on another murder investigation?"

"Looks that way."

"George isn't going to like it. You ever wonder if he'll be able to handle your help?"

"He is unhappy," I said. "But he also knows we can help. As long as we're careful and we tell him what we learn. If our relationship gets in the way, then that raises other issues."

. . .

THAT EVENING, the EB Eats Investigation Society reconvened at The Open Page. I shared everything Cleo had told me. Kashvi made notes and Jet pulled up search results on his tablet.

"So we're looking for a person who knew Amalia was investigating them," Kashvi said. "Someone with access to cyanide or the knowledge to obtain it. Someone who understood food chemistry well enough to mask the poison in chocolate. And someone desperate enough to commit murder rather than face exposure."

"That doesn't narrow it down much," Jet said. "Most of our suspects fit that profile. Do we know the results of the tests yet? It would help to know how the poison was delivered."

"Nope. And I don't think any officials are eager to share. Which is why we need to focus on motive," I said. "What exactly did each person have to lose? What was Amalia about to expose?"

"The timing means it came with the desserts." Anthone had been quiet until now. He wasn't an official member of the group, but his reputation was in danger, and a new chef needed to worry more about that. "Whoever did this had to know not only when Amalia would eat it, but how to introduce the poison without being detected. That requires specific knowledge—timing, technique, opportunity."

"So we look at who had access," Kashvi said.

"And who had the most to lose from Amalia's article," I added.

We divided up tasks for the next day. Jet would talk to his tour guide network and local vendors. Kashvi would dig into public records and professional histories. Anthone would analyze the food preparation and service, identifying when and how the poison could have been introduced. And

I would talk to more people who'd interacted with Amalia—festival participants, anyone who might have seen or heard something useful.

A twinge of guilt about not letting George or Denise know what we'd found didn't make me call. We had suspicion. They needed more than that to act on.

When I got home that night, Macchiato was waiting by the door. She looked at me like I was late, which I was.

"I know, I know," I said, scooping her up. "It's been a long day."

She allowed the cuddle for about thirty seconds before wriggling free and stalking toward her food bowl. I filled it, then collapsed on the couch with the notes I'd made.

Amalia Limonete. Fifty-one years old. Famous food critic with a reputation for brutal honesty—maybe not so much the honesty. Thinks she's an investigative journalist exposing something fishy in the food industry. Someone with enemies who'd found a way to silence her.

The question was: which enemy had been desperate enough to kill?

I thought about Hugo Delacroix and his stolen recipe, about Rajan Okoye and his clear dislike of the woman, about Octavia Beaumont and the way she hounded Amalia. Keiko Nakamura and how she must feel about the woman who destroyed her. I thought about Felix Kowalski and whatever Amalia had discovered about his business, about all the vendors who'd seemed nervous when she approached.

Too many people with a motive. One of them was a murderer.

And somehow, the EB Eats Investigation Society had to

figure out which one—before George's patience ran out, before the killer struck again, and before Nueva Vida's reputation was destroyed beyond repair.

Macchiato jumped onto my lap, purring. I stroked her soft fur and tried to organize my thoughts. Tomorrow we'd start asking questions. Tonight, I just needed to rest.

10

The Open Page had a comfortable clutter that suggested serious work was happening somewhere in the bookshelves. Kashvi had pushed aside displays of bestsellers to create a workspace at the reading nook, and now papers covered every available surface while her laptop glowed.

"I still don't like this," Cleo said, setting down a manila folder. "These were Amalia's private research files. She trusted me to keep them confidential."

"Amalia's dead," Jet pointed out. "And whoever killed her might have done it because of what's in those files."

I watched Cleo's shoulders tense. She'd agreed to help us, but I could see her mind changing as she handed us the evidence. We still needed that notebook, but Amalia had more than just her shorthand notes to work with.

"We're not going to publish anything," Kashvi said. "We just need to understand what Amalia was working on. What she might have threatened."

Cleo nodded, then flipped open the folder. "She was

building a comprehensive exposé of someone she suspected of corrupting the industry she loved."

Anthone leaned forward. "But we don't know who."

"I read up on some of the crimes that happen in the food services industry," Jet said.

"Every industry has bad people," Kashvi said.

I pulled the folder closer, scanning the organized documents. Amalia might have been caustic, but she was thorough. Each suspect had their own section, color-coded and cross-referenced. No names no details of this crime she wanted to stop. Everything was numbered. "She documented everything. Do you think the notebook has the key to decode this?"

"She was thorough." Cleo sat forward in her chair. "Amalia said the truth mattered more than being liked. That food critics had a responsibility to expose fraud. That's why everyone believed her when she gave a bad review."

Why did I think Amalia traded heavily on that reputation for being honest and rigorous?

Kashvi was already creating a spreadsheet on her laptop. "Let's go through these one by one. What did she have on each person? I'll leave a column blank for the name when we figure it out."

The first file made me wince. It was numbered forty-two and as thick with documentation—evidence going back seven years, pay offs for favorable reviews.

"This would end a career," Anthone said. "It could be Rajan, but there's no guarantee number forty-two is in Nueva Vida."

"How much money are we talking about?" Jet asked. "It won't help us figure out the answer, but it might make the motive stronger."

Cleo didn't hesitate. "It's not the fees. It's the future. The current book deal alone is worth two hundred thousand. Plus his existing books will be pulled so the royalties are gone. Then brand partnerships, the works. If this came out, publishers could sue for fraud. Whoever this is would lose everything."

We agreed to put Rajan's name in the spreadsheet with a question mark. Motive: financial ruin. Means: access to kitchen. Opportunity: present during tasting.

The familiar shape of an investigation was forming.

The next file was number seven, and it described a chef whose star had faded.

Kashvi read aloud: "Three failed restaurant ventures in five years. Investors pulling out. Previous show canceled due to low ratings. Network considering her for new competition series—pending Amalia's participation as lead judge. I might know who this is. Octavia."

"Wait." I looked up at Cleo. "Amalia was supposed to be on Octavia's show?"

"Not just on it. The show's entire concept depended on having a critic of Amalia's caliber." Cleo's voice was flat. "Octavia needed Amalia's credibility to make it work. Without that, the network would drop the project."

"So when Amalia refused..." Kashvi's fingers flew across her keyboard.

"Octavia's comeback dies before it starts," Jet finished. "That's desperate."

"People kill for less," I said. Sometimes desperation made monsters of ordinary people.

The number didn't make any connections pop into our minds, so we moved on. The next file didn't have a number. Just the word first. Could she make it more difficult to decipher?

Everything in the file made my stomach turn. Amalia

hadn't just documented this person's harassment—she'd traced the pattern of a "tell-all" book. Recipe theft disguised as memoir. Names changed just enough to avoid legal trouble, but anyone in the industry would recognize the chefs he was claiming to expose. "Hugo?"

Cleo leaned forward. "She truly hated him. Most people she just didn't care about. But Hugo got to her."

"It says he stole recipes, then wrote a book about being stolen from?" Jet's tone was incredulous.

"It's brilliant in a horrible way," Kashvi said. "Position yourself as the victim while profiting from your crimes."

Cleo nodded. "Amalia was going to expose the whole thing. Show that every 'secret recipe' in his book was stolen from someone else. She had documentation, witnesses, the works."

"But it's not a crime," Anthone said. "Yeah, it's morally questionable, but is it a motive? Mostly chefs just cite the inspiration and tweak a bit. "

I wrote down the details, my hand moving while my mind wrestled with the implications. Hugo's harassment made more sense now—attack before being attacked. Discredit the critic before she could discredit him.

The next section made me pause. Unlike the others, this wasn't about personal corruption. Amalia had been investigating a family business—health code violations covered up through political connections, suspicious sourcing practices, underpaid migrant workers.

"This is different," I said, looking at Cleo. "This would destroy more than a reputation."

"It would destroy a family's legacy." Cleo's voice was quiet. "If I had to guess, this sounds like Felix. Four generations of restaurants. His father built that empire, and Felix has been trying to clean up the mess he inherited. But Amalia threatened to publish everything—make it look like Felix was personally responsible for all of it."

Kashvi frowned. "Was he?"

"I don't know. Mostly it was before Felix inherited. Amalia's research was solid, but she wasn't interested in nuance. Guilty by association was enough for her."

The bookstore door opened, bringing in a rush of cool air and a young man I recognized from the festival. Tall, early thirties, with Hugo's aristocratic nose and worried eyes.

"Knox said I might find you here," he said, looking at me. "I'm Amos Delacroix. Hugo's son."

The silence that followed was awkward. I gestured to an empty chair. "Please, sit down."

"I heard the police are investigating my father for murder?" Amos settled into the chair. "Knox told me about your team. Said you were trying to figure out what really happened to Amalia."

"Do you have something to tell us?" I asked. I didn't want to hope this young man had the key to the code.

"Everything about this situation is wrong." Amos ran a hand through his hair. "Look, I know my father can be difficult. But he's not a killer. His harassment of Amalia was wrong, I told him so myself, but murder? That's not who he is. He's just passionate about everything."

Jet leaned against the bookshelf. "You don't think he'd take action? Even to protect his reputation?"

"Dad's reputation has survived worse. He thrives on controversy—any publicity is good publicity, you know?" Amos's voice carried the exhaustion of someone who'd defended his father too many times. "But La Maison

Delacroix is different. That restaurant is his legacy, what he wants to leave me."

"So you had motive too," Anthone said.

"I had motive to stop her, yes. But I was planning to do that with lawyers, not cyanide. And I was doing it for dad." Amos met our eyes. "I don't want the restaurant. I'm a banker. Dad never believed it. I want you to investigate. I want the truth out there, whatever it is. Because right now, everyone assumes it was dad, and that shadow will follow our restaurant forever."

We assured Amos we were going to find the killer. His expression said he didn't buy it, but he nodded and headed out. Cleo checked her phone and followed him.

We spent the next while organizing information, creating connections on Kashvi's digital version of what would become our investigation board. Names, motives, timelines—everything laid out in color-coded precision.

What we guessed was Birdie's file emerged as particularly interesting. Her entire influencer brand was built on authentic food experiences and supporting struggling chefs, but Amalia had documentation of paid promotions that were presented as surprise finds.

"It's not unusual," I said. "Most shows, or blogs get paid for reviews. It's considered advertising. I'm not sure what we have here rises to more than an annoyance.

I looked at the growing web of connections. "So we have Rajan facing exposure for fraudulent reviews. Octavia needing Amalia's participation for her career comeback. Hugo's tell-all book about to be revealed as recipe theft. Felix's family business investigation. Birdie's influencer fraud." I paused. "That's five people with desperate motives."

"Six if you count Amos protecting his father and the restaurant legacy," Jet said.

The conversation wound down as afternoon light shifted through the bookstore windows.

I gathered my notes, feeling the weight of too much information and not enough clarity. "We're not closer to an answer, are we? In fact, we're really just guessing about the identities of the people in her files."

"We're closer to understanding the question," Kashvi said. "This wasn't about revenge for a bad review. This was about prevention."

"Someone killed her before she could destroy them," Jet agreed.

The thought followed me home, where Macchiato greeted me with her usual enthusiastic meowing. I fed her first—a cat's needs were simple and immediate, a welcome contrast to the day's complexities.

Then I turned to cooking, because my hands needed something familiar. Chicken enchiladas, the kind of comfort food that required attention but not complicated technique. I roasted fresh Hatch chilies over the gas flame, turning them with tongs until the skins blistered and blackened. The smoky scent filled the kitchen—sharp and bright and grounding. I sealed them in a paper bag to steam, then shredded rotisserie chicken while they cooled.

Macchiato wove between my ankles, purring. I'd named her after my favorite coffee drink, though her personality was more espresso than macchiato—intense and demanding. But right now, her presence was what I needed.

I peeled the chilies, their skins slipping off in charred sheets. Chopped them fine, mixed them with cream and chicken stock and a touch of cumin. The sauce needed to simmer, so I started rolling tortillas—chicken, cheese, a spoonful of sauce, all tucked tight and arranged in the baking dish. Layer after layer until the pan was full.

The repetitive work cleared my head. Pour the remaining sauce over the top. More cheese. Slide it into the oven.

As the enchiladas baked, I sat at my small kitchen table with a glass of wine and my notes. Amalia Limonete had been building an exposé that would destroy careers, expose fraud, and damage family legacies. Some of her targets probably deserved it—recipe theft, consumer fraud, industry corruption. But others were more complicated. Felix trying to fix his family's problems. Birdie's influencer marketing that crossed ethical lines but wasn't exactly criminal.

Amalia had seen everything in black and white. Truth versus lies, authentic versus fraud. But life wasn't that simple. People were messy and complicated, and sometimes the line between justice and revenge was thinner than we wanted to believe.

Macchiato leaped from the floor to my lap, kneading my thigh with her claws and purring. I scratched behind her ears, feeling some of the tension ease.

The oven timer dinged. I retrieved the enchiladas, their cheese bubbling and golden. Made myself a plate, topped it with fresh cilantro and a dollop of sour cream. Sat back down with Macchiato supervising from the chair next to mine.

The food was exactly what I needed—comforting, familiar, grounding. Each bite reminded me why I'd opened EB Eats, why I'd chosen this life. Food as connection, as comfort, as home.

But it also reminded me that even comfort could be

complicated. Amalia had exposed frauds in the food industry, people lying to customers and profiting from deception. That was wrong. But she'd also been willing to destroy people who were trying to do better, to paint everyone with the same brush of judgment.

11

The morning rush had slowed when Cleo walked into EB Eats. She looked ten years older than she had two days ago. I poured her coffee and set it down without a word.

"I couldn't sleep," she said. "Keep thinking about what was in that notebook."

Kashvi had been drinking coffee at the counter. She leaned forward. "What did Amalia keep in it?"

Cleo took a breath. "Everything. Every interview, every piece of evidence, every vulnerability she'd found. She showed me some of it a few weeks ago, wanted my opinion on whether she had enough to publish." She stared into her coffee. "I told her she did. I told her it would be the exposé of the decade."

I refilled her mug.

"There were side-by-side recipe comparisons proving Rajan stole dishes from an unpublished manuscript he reviewed for a small press. The original chef died two years ago, never knowing his life's work would become someone else's signature menu. Amalia had the manuscript, Rajan's published recipes, even email exchanges where he dismissed the work as amateurish while copying it word for word. Same with a lot of his reviews."

"No bookstore would carry his books if it came out." Kashvi pulled out her phone and started taking notes. "That's definitely plagiarism. Career-ending."

"It gets worse." Cleo's voice dropped. "She had documentation on Octavia too. Raw footage from her show's production company proving she manufactures drama, edits conversations to create conflicts that never happened, stages surprise revelations contestants were briefed on days before. One chef quit the industry after what they did to him on camera."

I thought about Octavia's television smile. "How did Amalia get production footage?"

"A whistleblower. Someone who couldn't stomach the manipulation anymore." Cleo looked up at us. "Amalia had names, dates, specific episodes. She was going to publish it all in a series of articles, starting next month. The first one was already written."

The bell over the door rang. Jet walked in with Anthone behind him.

"Coffee?" I asked.

"And information," Jet said, sliding onto a stool. "We need to talk about that notebook."

"We already are." I nodded toward Cleo. "She's been telling us what Amalia documented."

Anthone listened as Cleo repeated everything. When she finished, he let out a low whistle.

"He seemed so nice," he said. "Maybe in contrast to Amalia he came across as way nicer than he is."

"Octavia's show is her entire brand," Kashvi added. "Without it, she's nothing. If that footage went public, the production company would drop her."

"I'm not so sure about that," I said. "Isn't all reality TV edited to make people look worse than they are?"

Jet drummed his fingers on the counter. "So we've got multiple people who needed that notebook to disappear. Question is, did one of them kill Amalia to get it?"

"Or did someone take advantage of the murder to steal it afterward?" I topped up my coffee. "We need to find out who was near that area between when Amalia died and when the police secured the scene."

Cleo shook her head. "I don't know. Everything was chaos. People were running around, trying to see what was happening. It could have been anyone."

"Then we need to work this from different angles." I looked around at my friends. "Jet, can you try to get the festival security footage? See if we can track who went near the center?"

"Yeah, already asked my buddy. He said George already has a copy, but no one told him not to make more. We should have it this afternoon."

"Kashvi, what if you dig into the online trail? Rajan, Octavia, Hugo, anyone else who might have had something to lose. See if there's anything public that connects to what Amalia was investigating."

"On it." Kashvi was typing on her phone. "I'll use the bookstore as my base. I can't expect Mallory to drop her courses to help out full time. And people know I'm there. Gossip flows a bit more readily over a romance or cozy mystery."

I turned to Anthone. "You know the local chef community better than any of us. Can you reach out to some contacts, see if anyone knows about this plagiarism situation? Or if there were other issues Amalia might have uncovered?"

"I'll make some calls," he agreed. "A lot of chefs pass through Nueva Vida during festival season. Someone might know something. And I need to make the contacts anyway. If I ever get serious about my own business."

"What about me?" Cleo asked.

"You need to rest," I said. "And if Detective Kramer wants to talk to you again, you need to be clear-headed."

She nodded. "Call me if you learn anything?"

"Yes." I kept the qualifier of 'if I can' unsaid.

After Cleo left, we sat in silence for a moment.

The lunch rush started filtering in. As I moved between tables, delivering blue corn pancakes and tortilla pie, I listened for any juicy topics to join in on.

Martha and her book club were dissecting the case over chicken tortilla soup. I suppose we weren't the only ones who felt a need to solve a murder.

"I heard that Rajan person left the festival grounds right after his demonstration," Mrs. Waverly was saying. "Drove all the way back to Albuquerque and didn't return until the next morning."

"How would anyone know that?" Martha asked.

"I got ears, and I'm not so old I lost the use of them. My great nephew works at the hotel. Said he was furious about something and couldn't stand to stay."

I refilled their water glasses. "How's the soup?"

"Delicious, as always, dear." Martha patted my hand. "You know, it's terrible what happened to that critic. She ate here two nights before, didn't she?"

"She did. Had the posole. Just like a regular diner, no critique."

Martha gave me a look that told me she knew I was holding back. "Don't pretend you aren't looking for clues. Now you look back, did she seem worried about anything?"

I thought about it. "She seemed focused. Like she had a lot on her mind."

I joined Kashvi at the counter where she was waiting for her takeout order.

"Learn anything?" I asked.

"Rajan's social media went completely dark the day after Amalia died," she said. "No posts, no stories, nothing. His restaurant's accounts are still active, but his personal ones? Silent."

"Could just be grief. They worked together for years."

"Maybe. But I found something else." She opened her notebook. "Three months ago, there was a cease-and-desist letter filed in Santa Fe. A small publisher claimed someone plagiarized their manuscript. The records didn't name anyone, and the case was settled quietly."

"You think it was Rajan?"

"The timing matches when Amalia started her research. And the publisher specializes in culinary manuscripts from working chefs." Kashvi tapped her screen. "Want to bet one of those manuscripts belonged to the chef whose recipes Rajan stole?"

Before I could answer, Anthone came through the kitchen entrance, phone still in his hand.

"Got something," he said. "One of my chef friends worked a competition with Rajan last year. Said Rajan got into a screaming match with one of the judges about recipe attribution. Claimed someone was trying to discredit him with baseless plagiarism accusations."

"Last year?" I frowned. "So this wasn't new."

"No. Which means Rajan knew someone was onto him long before Amalia died." Anthone grabbed a tortilla chip from the basket I kept under the counter. "If she had actual proof, documentation he couldn't deny, that's a strong motive."

Jet arrived just as the dinner rush was dying down. He was carrying his laptop.

"Kashvi's just closing the store. The security footage came through," he announced. "And you're going to want to see this."

We crowded around his screen.

"This is the angle that shows the front and side entrance to the community center," he said, forwarding through several hours of footage. "Here's when people start arriving in the morning, setting up. There's Amalia, going in around eight. Cleo brings her coffee at eight-thirty."

Kashvi joined us just as we started watching the sped-up footage. It showed the normal flow of the festival day. Then Jet slowed it down.

"Here. Eleven-forty. See that person?"

A figure in a dark jacket and baseball cap approached the side door of the community center, glanced around, then slipped inside. Too far away to make out a face.

"Could be anyone," Kashvi said.

"Wait." Jet forwarded the footage. "They're in there for three minutes. Then they come out, and look what they're carrying."

The figure emerged with something tucked under their jacket. Something roughly the size of a notebook.

"That's before Amalia died," I said. "The cyanide wouldn't have taken effect yet."

"Right. So either this person took the notebook while Amalia was still alive, maybe while she was already feeling sick and couldn't stop them..." Jet paused. "Or this is the killer, and they took it right after delivering the poison."

We stared at the frozen frame, trying to make out any identifying features. The person had their face turned away from the camera, aware of its location.

"Someone who knows festival security," Kashvi said. "Who would know where the cameras are."

"Or someone who's been to enough festivals to be aware of standard setup," Anthone countered. "Could still be any of our suspects."

I thought about what we'd learned today. Rajan with his stolen recipes and reviews, knowing Amalia had proof that would destroy him. Octavia and her manipulated footage, her entire career built on manufactured drama. Hugo, who'd admitted his family's pastries were copied but who might have more to hide than he'd claimed.

"We need to work out who this person is," I said. "Can you get the footage enhanced, Jet? Maybe get a clearer image?"

"I can try. Might take a day or two." He closed his laptop. "In the meantime, we keep digging."

"And we're careful," Kashvi warned. "We're dealing with someone who's already killed once. If they figure out we're investigating..."

"Then we make sure they don't." I looked at my friends. "Unless we know we can trust the person, we keep our questions casual, our interest neighborly. Just concerned citizens of Nueva Vida who want to know what happened."

Chapter 12

The Nueva Vida Community Center smelled like caramelized onions and roasted garlic when Kashvi and I arrived Saturday afternoon. Rajan Okoye stood at the front of the demonstration kitchen, dicing shallots. About thirty people filled the folding chairs, most clutching the new cookbook he'd been signing earlier.

His bow tie today was deep purple with tiny golden spoons scattered across it, paired with burgundy suspenders over a crisp white oxford. Even cooking, he looked like he'd stepped out of a food magazine.

"The key to a proper French onion soup," he said as we took seats near the back, "is patience. You cannot rush the caramelization process. Good cooking, like good writing, requires you to respect the time each element needs to develop its full potential."

I caught Kashvi's eye. We'd come to talk to Rajan about Amalia's investigation, but watching him work was something else. His hands moved like he'd forgotten anyone was watching, and his commentary wove together technique, history, and cultural context in a way that made even basic knife skills feel important.

"Now, many people think French onion soup is purely French," he continued, adding butter to a heavy pot. "But the truth is more complicated. Every culture has its version of cooked onions in broth. The genius is in how we borrow from each other, how we transform shared ingredients into something new while acknowledging the foundations we build upon."

He glanced up, and our eyes met. Recognition crossed his face, followed by what I interpreted as resignation. He knew why we were here.

"Cultural exchange in food is a delicate thing," he said, holding my gaze. "There's a line between appreciation and appropriation, between building on traditions and stealing them. The best food writers understand that line."

The audience murmured, probably thinking this was planned commentary. But I heard the message. He was willing to talk, just maybe not here in front of thirty witnesses and a local cable channel camera crew.

We sat through the rest of the demonstration. The onions caramelized into deep amber sweetness swimming in rich beef broth under a blanket of melted Gruyère. Rajan answered questions with the same authority he'd shown throughout, recommending variations for vegetarians, discussing the best bread for croutons, explaining why low-sodium broth gave you better flavor control.

"Food brings us together," he said as people started gathering their things. "Even when everything else divides us, we can still share a meal and find common ground."

As the crowd dispersed, Kashvi approached the demonstration table while I hung back. Rajan cleaned his workspace with the same care he'd shown while cooking, wiping down surfaces and organizing his tools.

"Impressive," Kashvi said. "The soup smells incredible."

"Thank you." He didn't look up from scrubbing the cutting board. "I assume you're not here for cooking tips, though."

"Cleo gave us Amalia's records," I said. "We know about the plagiarism investigation."

His hands stopped for a moment before resuming their circles. "I wondered when that would surface. Small town, big secrets—everything comes out eventually." He looked up. "Though I was hoping for a few more days of pretending my career wasn't about to implode."

"Want to tell us your side?" I asked. "We're trying to understand who might have wanted Amalia silenced."

"You must know I'm not unique." It wasn't a question.

"Yes, we're talking to everyone who had something to lose from her investigations," Kashvi said. "We're not here to judge. Well, not entirely. We're here to understand."

Rajan set down the scrubber and leaned against the counter. The professional facade cracked, revealing something raw underneath. "You want the childhood trauma that led to food obsession, or should we skip straight to the part where I became a literary thief?"

"Start wherever you're comfortable," I said.

He was quiet for a moment, then reached for one of the leftover bowls of soup. "My family came to the States from Nigeria when I was eight. My father was an engineer—brilliant man who could speak four languages and design bridges that would stand for centuries. But his degree wasn't worth anything here. We went from middle-class comfort to him working three jobs."

Too familiar a story to be a motive, I thought. Then another little voice said that being common didn't reduce the pain.

"Food became complicated for us," Rajan continued. "Sometimes there wasn't enough. Sometimes there was nothing."

"I can't imagine," Kashvi said.

"It teaches you things. About scarcity. About what you'll do to survive." He started portioning the leftover soup into containers. "When I discovered food writing, it felt like magic. I could eat at amazing restaurants, learn about cuisines from around the world, and get paid for it. Suddenly I had access to a world where food was abundant, celebrated, transformed into art."

"And you wanted to be part of that world," I said.

"Desperately. I would have done anything." He sealed one container and reached for another. "At first, I was just trying to sound more educated than I was. It worked. People took my reviews seriously because I sounded like I knew what I was talking about."

"That's not a crime," Kashvi said. "There's something else, right?"

"It started innocently enough." He lined up the containers. "Someone offered me a fee to give them a review. It's done all the time. Like Ad spending."

I remember the same comment about Birdie getting paid for her influencer posts. It couldn't be the motive if paying was normal. While I though, I watched him work, noting the care he took even with something as simple as storing leftover soup. There was real skill in how he moved through a kitchen, genuine knowledge in how he talked about food. Which made his theft worse—he'd had something real to offer and had poisoned it with lies.

"Then a big celebrity chef asked me to make it a glowing review," he continued. "He hiked up the fee. I rationalize it as getting paid for something I would do anyway. A celebrity chef wouldn't dare offer substandard food."

"Isn't that unethical?" I found myself imaging the tiny steps he took into the gray area.

"Yes. But my justification worked for a while. These were all restaurants I'd give excellent recommendations." His shoulders rose. "Then one well-known chef offered me more money. I didn't know at the time she was about to be exposed for exploiting her staff. Her bad press came out the same day as my review. People paid no attention to the claims of her cooks."

"People were hurt by that," Kashvi said. "But you didn't stop, right?"

"No. It was too much money. Every time I thought of turning down an... arrangement, I remembered being hungry."

I understood how a difficult past could color the present, but with that one review, he crossed a line. "And if Amalia exposed you? What would happen?"

"My book deals would be canceled. Magazine would drop me." He started wiping down the stove. "That's when I realized the fear that I'd go back to not knowing where my next meal came from made me a stupid man."

I'd been prepared to feel simple anger at his actions, but the reality was messier. Rajan understood what he'd done, and his guilt seemed real. Which didn't make it better, but it made him human.

"We heard you arguing with Amalia the day before she died," I said. "Not just us, there were plenty of people around."

He scrubbed at a spot on the stove. "I was trying to convince her that I would get help. That I wouldn't do it again. I'd be more critical."

"She didn't believe you," Kashvi said.

"It was devastating. She was right about everything, and I knew it, and I still couldn't admit it publicly because that would mean..." He trailed off, setting down the cloth. "It would mean acknowledging that my entire career was a fraud."

"But you're willing to admit it now," I observed.

"Now that she's dead and her investigation is going forward anyway?" He shook his head. "This isn't nobility. This is just accepting the inevitable. With Amalia gone, her assistant has all the evidence. Her nephew is handling her estate. The truth will come out regardless."

"What about the cooks you dismissed as unimportant?" I asked. "What do they deserve?"

He was quiet for long enough to worry me, staring at his reflection in the polished stove surface. "Everything. An apology. Someone on their side. This industry can be so exploitive. I could have helped." He turned to face us. "I've been thinking about reaching out to them, trying to make some kind of amends. Though I'm not sure forgiveness is possible after this."

"It's a start, though," Kashvi said.

"Maybe. If I survive the fallout." He managed a smile, sad but real. "Though I suppose surviving career destruction is better than what happened to Amalia."

I couldn't argue with that.

"Walk us through the festival timeline," I said. "We know there wasn't much time between her taking in the poison and dying. But not how it got into her system."

"Signing books at the Williams Gallery booth for most of the afternoon. My new cookbook just came out—one of the few things I wrote myself, though now nobody will believe that." He pulled out his phone and showed us photos with timestamps. "I was there from two until almost four-thirty. Plenty of witnesses, several photos with readers."

Kashvi made a few notes before asking, "Did you interact with Amalia again after your argument?"

"I saw her at the judges' table, but we didn't speak. I was avoiding her at that point." He pocketed his phone. "Look, I know how this looks. Strong motive, access to the festival area. I didn't kill her; I was planning to do the one thing scarier than murder—I was going to confess publicly before she could expose me."

"Really?" Kashvi asked. "It seems pretty convenient timing."

"I'd drafted the statement that morning. Apology to the cooks, to my readers, a promise to make restitution." He pulled out his phone again and showed us a notes app entry dated the morning of Amalia's death. "I figured if I controlled the narrative, admitted everything before she published, maybe I could salvage some scrap of dignity from the wreckage."

I read through the statement. It was thorough, unflinching in its admission of guilt, and devastating in its acknowledgment of harm done. It was also unsent. I could picture Rajan's smile and charm getting him off the hook.

"Why didn't you publish it?" I asked.

"Cowardice. Fear. The hope that maybe I could talk Amalia into giving me more time." He laughed without humor. "She wasn't the negotiating type. But I thought I could explain, make her understand how desperate I was, how much I loved the food culture I'd been writing about..."

We spent another twenty minutes going through details. His interactions with other suspects. Rajan painted a picture of a food industry where everyone carried secrets, where the pressure to maintain authenticity while producing new content pushed people toward desperate measures. A very different life to the one I knew. "It's not too late to start over," I said when we had our answers. "To write about your own experiences."

"Maybe. If anyone still wants to read my work after this." He handed me one of the containers of soup. "Here. It's my grandmother's recipe, I got it when she was teaching me to cook."

Outside, the late afternoon sun painted Nueva Vida's adobe buildings in warm gold. The scent of sage and piñon smoke drifted from someone's fireplace, and I could hear laughter from the plaza where tourists were photographing the old mission church.

"So," Kashvi said as we walked toward EB Eats. "What's your professional amateur sleuth opinion?"

"That he's telling the truth about the plagiarism and being terrified of exposure." I shifted the warm soup container. "But whether we heard the truth about planning to confess about that instead of murder..."

She looked around as if she thought we were under surveillance. "He has a strong motive. His career was built on lies."

"But did he have the opportunity?" I thought about the timeline. "His alibi for the signing is solid, and the poisoning had to happen during a specific window. Plus there's something about him that doesn't feel like a murderer."

"You mean like a decent person who made terrible choices?" Kashvi's voice carried a load of cynicism.

"Exactly." We paused at the corner. "Rajan seems more likely to publicly confess and beg forgiveness than risk murder charges. The guilt is eating him alive."

"I don't know. He talks like that, but I don't see evidence of him actually doing anything. And none of that rules him out," Kashvi said. "Being a first generation American is hard no matter what happens. Decent people can do desperate things when they're cornered, but do they deserve lenience?"

"True." I thought about how confident he'd been in the demonstration kitchen. "Someone with his training would know exactly how to disguise cyanide even if it wasn't in food."

She shook her head at the facts. "But would he risk it at a public festival? With witnesses everywhere?"

"Maybe that was the point. Make it look like an accident, a tragic coincidence." I shifted the soup. "Or maybe I'm overthinking this because I want him to be innocent. He gave me his grandmother's soup to try."

"Eliza Burton, sucker for sentimental food stories," Kashvi teased. "I'm not sure I'd eat anything a suspect prepared."

12

The Nueva Vida Community Center smelled like caramelized onions and roasted garlic when Kashvi and I arrived Saturday afternoon. Rajan Okoye stood at the front of the demonstration kitchen, dicing shallots. About thirty people filled the folding chairs, most clutching the new cookbook he'd been signing earlier.

His bow tie today was deep purple with tiny golden spoons scattered across it, paired with burgundy suspenders over a crisp white oxford. Even cooking, he looked like he'd stepped out of a food magazine.

"The key to a proper French onion soup," he said as we took seats near the back, "is patience. You cannot rush the caramelization process. Good cooking, like good writing, requires you to respect the time each element needs to develop its full potential."

I caught Kashvi's eye. We'd come to talk to Rajan about Amalia's investigation, but watching him work was something else. His hands moved like he'd forgotten anyone was watching, and his commentary wove together technique, history, and cultural context in a way that made even basic knife skills feel important.

"Now, many people think French onion soup is purely French," he continued, adding butter to a heavy pot. "But the truth is more complicated. Every culture has its version of cooked onions in broth. The genius is in how we borrow from each other, how we transform shared ingredients into something new while acknowledging the foundations we build upon."

He glanced up, and our eyes met. Recognition crossed his face, followed by what I interpreted as resignation. He knew why we were here.

"Cultural exchange in food is a delicate thing," he said, holding my gaze. "There's a line between appreciation and appropriation, between building on traditions and stealing them. The best food writers understand that line."

The audience murmured, probably thinking this was planned commentary. But I heard the message. He was willing to talk, just maybe not here in front of thirty witnesses and a local cable channel camera crew.

We sat through the rest of the demonstration. The onions caramelized into deep amber sweetness swimming in rich beef broth under a blanket of melted Gruyère. Rajan answered questions with the same authority he'd shown throughout, recommending variations for vegetarians, discussing the best bread for croutons, explaining why low-sodium broth gave you better flavor control.

"Food brings us together," he said as people started gathering their things. "Even when everything else divides us, we can still share a meal and find common ground."

As the crowd dispersed, Kashvi approached the demonstration table while I hung back. Rajan cleaned his workspace with the same care he'd shown while cooking, wiping down surfaces and organizing his tools.

"Impressive," Kashvi said. "The soup smells incredible."

"Thank you." He didn't look up from scrubbing the cutting board. "I assume you're not here for cooking tips, though."

"Cleo gave us Amalia's records," I said. "We know about the plagiarism investigation."

His hands stopped for a moment before resuming their circles. "I wondered when that would surface. Small town, big secrets—everything comes out eventually." He looked up. "Though I was hoping for a few more days of pretending my career wasn't about to implode."

"Want to tell us your side?" I asked. "We're trying to understand who might have wanted Amalia silenced."

"You must know I'm not unique." It wasn't a question.

"Yes, we're talking to everyone who had something to lose from her investigations," Kashvi said. "We're not here to judge. Well, not entirely. We're here to understand."

Rajan set down the scrubber and leaned against the counter. The professional facade cracked, revealing something raw underneath. "You want the childhood trauma that led to food obsession, or should we skip straight to the part where I became a literary thief?"

"Start wherever you're comfortable," I said.

He was quiet for a moment, then reached for one of the leftover bowls of soup. "My family came to the States from Nigeria when I was eight. My father was an engineer—brilliant man who could speak four languages and design bridges that would stand for centuries. But his degree wasn't worth anything here. We went from middle-class comfort to him working three jobs."

Too familiar a story to be a motive, I thought. Then

another little voice said that being common didn't reduce the pain.

"Food became complicated for us," Rajan continued. "Sometimes there wasn't enough. Sometimes there was nothing."

"I can't imagine," Kashvi said.

"It teaches you things. About scarcity. About what you'll do to survive." He started portioning the leftover soup into containers. "When I discovered food writing, it felt like magic. I could eat at amazing restaurants, learn about cuisines from around the world, and get paid for it. Suddenly I had access to a world where food was abundant, celebrated, transformed into art."

"And you wanted to be part of that world," I said.

"Desperately. I would have done anything." He sealed one container and reached for another. "At first, I was just trying to sound more educated than I was. It worked. People took my reviews seriously because I sounded like I knew what I was talking about."

"That's not a crime," Kashvi said. "There's something else, right?"

"It started innocently enough." He lined up the containers. "Someone offered me a fee to give them a review. It's done all the time. Like Ad spending."

I remember the same comment about Birdie getting paid for her influencer posts. It couldn't be the motive if paying was normal. While I though, I watched him work, noting the care he took even with something as simple as storing leftover soup. There was real skill in how he moved through a kitchen, genuine knowledge in how he talked about food. Which made his theft worse—he'd had something real to offer and had poisoned it with lies.

"Then a big celebrity chef asked me to make it a

glowing review," he continued. "He hiked up the fee. I rationalize it as getting paid for something I would do anyway. A celebrity chef wouldn't dare offer substandard food."

"Isn't that unethical?" I found myself imaging the tiny steps he took into the gray area.

"Yes. But my justification worked for a while. These were all restaurants I'd give excellent recommendations." His shoulders rose. "Then one well-known chef offered me more money. I didn't know at the time she was about to be exposed for exploiting her staff. Her bad press came out the same day as my review. People paid no attention to the claims of her cooks."

"People were hurt by that," Kashvi said. "But you didn't stop, right?"

"No. It was too much money. Every time I thought of turning down an... arrangement, I remembered being hungry."

I understood how a difficult past could color the present, but with that one review, he crossed a line. "And if Amalia exposed you? What would happen?"

"My book deals would be canceled. Magazine would drop me." He started wiping down the stove. "That's when I realized the fear that I'd go back to not knowing where my next meal came from made me a stupid man."

I'd been prepared to feel simple anger at his actions, but the reality was messier. Rajan understood what he'd done, and his guilt seemed real. Which didn't make it better, but it made him human.

"We heard you arguing with Amalia the day before she died," I said. "Not just us, there were plenty of people around."

He scrubbed at a spot on the stove. "I was trying to

convince her that I would get help. That I wouldn't do it again. I'd be more critical."

"She didn't believe you," Kashvi said.

"It was devastating. She was right about everything, and I knew it, and I still couldn't admit it publicly because that would mean..." He trailed off, setting down the cloth. "It would mean acknowledging that my entire career was a fraud."

"But you're willing to admit it now," I observed.

"Now that she's dead and her investigation is going forward anyway?" He shook his head. "This isn't nobility. This is just accepting the inevitable. With Amalia gone, her assistant has all the evidence. Her nephew is handling her estate. The truth will come out regardless."

"What about the cooks you dismissed as unimportant?" I asked. "What do they deserve?"

He was quiet for long enough to worry me, staring at his reflection in the polished stove surface. "Everything. An apology. Someone on their side. This industry can be so exploitive. I could have helped." He turned to face us. "I've been thinking about reaching out to them, trying to make some kind of amends. Though I'm not sure forgiveness is possible after this."

"It's a start, though," Kashvi said.

"Maybe. If I survive the fallout." He managed a smile, sad but real. "Though I suppose surviving career destruction is better than what happened to Amalia."

I couldn't argue with that.

"Walk us through the festival timeline," I said. "We know there wasn't much time between her taking in the poison and dying. But not how it got into her system."

"Signing books at the Williams Gallery booth for most of the afternoon. My new cookbook just came out—one of the few things I wrote myself, though now nobody will believe that." He pulled out his phone and showed us photos with timestamps. "I was there from two until almost four-thirty. Plenty of witnesses, several photos with readers."

Kashvi made a few notes before asking, "Did you interact with Amalia again after your argument?"

"I saw her at the judges' table, but we didn't speak. I was avoiding her at that point." He pocketed his phone. "Look, I know how this looks. Strong motive, access to the festival area. I didn't kill her; I was planning to do the one thing scarier than murder—I was going to confess publicly before she could expose me."

"Really?" Kashvi asked. "It seems pretty convenient timing."

"I'd drafted the statement that morning. Apology to the cooks, to my readers, a promise to make restitution." He pulled out his phone again and showed us a notes app entry dated the morning of Amalia's death. "I figured if I controlled the narrative, admitted everything before she published, maybe I could salvage some scrap of dignity from the wreckage."

I read through the statement. It was thorough, unflinching in its admission of guilt, and devastating in its acknowledgment of harm done. It was also unsent. I could picture Rajan's smile and charm getting him off the hook.

"Why didn't you publish it?" I asked.

"Cowardice. Fear. The hope that maybe I could talk Amalia into giving me more time." He laughed without humor. "She wasn't the negotiating type. But I thought I could explain, make her understand how desperate I was, how much I loved the food culture I'd been writing about..."

We spent another twenty minutes going through details. His interactions with other suspects. Rajan painted a picture of a food industry where everyone carried secrets, where the pressure to maintain authenticity while producing new content pushed people toward desperate measures. A very different life to the one I knew. "It's not too late to start over," I said when we had our answers. "To write about your own experiences."

"Maybe. If anyone still wants to read my work after this." He handed me one of the containers of soup. "Here. It's my grandmother's recipe, I got it when she was teaching me to cook."

Outside, the late afternoon sun painted Nueva Vida's adobe buildings in warm gold. The scent of sage and piñon smoke drifted from someone's fireplace, and I could hear laughter from the plaza where tourists were photographing the old mission church.

"So," Kashvi said as we walked toward EB Eats. "What's your professional amateur sleuth opinion?"

"That he's telling the truth about the plagiarism and being terrified of exposure." I shifted the warm soup container. "But whether we heard the truth about planning to confess about that instead of murder..."

She looked around as if she thought we were under surveillance. "He has a strong motive. His career was built on lies."

"But did he have the opportunity?" I thought about the timeline. "His alibi for the signing is solid, and the poisoning had to happen during a specific window. Plus there's something about him that doesn't feel like a murderer."

"You mean like a decent person who made terrible choices?" Kashvi's voice carried a load of cynicism.

"Exactly." We paused at the corner. "Rajan seems more

likely to publicly confess and beg forgiveness than risk murder charges. The guilt is eating him alive."

"I don't know. He talks like that, but I don't see evidence of him actually doing anything. And none of that rules him out," Kashvi said. "Being a first generation American is hard no matter what happens. Decent people can do desperate things when they're cornered, but do they deserve lenience?"

"True." I thought about how confident he'd been in the demonstration kitchen. "Someone with his training would know exactly how to disguise cyanide even if it wasn't in food."

She shook her head at the facts. "But would he risk it at a public festival? With witnesses everywhere?"

"Maybe that was the point. Make it look like an accident, a tragic coincidence." I shifted the soup. "Or maybe I'm overthinking this because I want him to be innocent. He gave me his grandmother's soup to try."

"Eliza Burton, sucker for sentimental food stories," Kashvi teased. "I'm not sure I'd eat anything a suspect prepared."

13

"No, no—curve your fingers back." Keiko Nakamura reached across the prep station and adjusted the girl's hand on the cutting board. "Knuckles forward, fingertips back. The knife should only touch your knuckles, never your fingers."

I watched as Keiko guided the student through proper knife technique. Even teaching at a festival booth, she moved like someone who'd spent decades in professional kitchens.

George hadn't closed down the festival so there was a lot of action going on. And I guessed he hoped letting the booths go one would keep his suspects close. If the festival ended, Nueva Vida would lose important tourist money, and the out-of-town participants would move on.

"Better." Keiko released the girl's hand. "Now try again. Slow and steady. Speed comes later."

We'd found her at one of the festival's demonstration areas, running a knife skills workshop for culinary students. The banner behind her read "Second Chances Kitchen" in cheerful letters. The exhaustion on Keiko's face told a different story.

"Ms. Nakamura?" I approached as the student continued chopping. "I'm Eliza Burton. This is Kashvi Verma and Anthone Sheret. We wanted to ask you about Amalia."

Keiko's knife hand paused—just for a second. She set down the chef's knife and turned to face us.

"I'm guessing this isn't about her reviewing my workshop." Her voice was level.

"We wanted to talk about your history with her," Kashvi said. "We understand she reviewed your restaurant. Sage and Smoke?"

Keiko glanced at her students, then gestured toward the side of the booth where a prep table held ingredients for her next demonstration.

"Keep practicing, everyone," she called to the group. "Remember—let the knife do the work."

She led us to the prep table and began sorting fresh herbs. Her hands moved on autopilot, separating cilantro from parsley, trimming stems. I recognized the need to keep busy, to anchor yourself in familiar work.

"Sage and Smoke closed five years ago," Keiko said. "Three months after Amalia's review ran."

"We read it," I said. "It seemed harsh."

Keiko's hands stopped moving. When she looked up, her eyes were hard. "Harsh?" The word came out on a hiss of anger. "She called my signature dish an affront to Southwestern cuisine. Said my fusion approach was culinary colonialism masquerading as innovation. Suggested I should stick to whatever cuisine my ancestors actually understood."

Hearing the facts made it hard to understand why Amalia was so successful. She'd appointed herself the savior of cultures—other people's cultures. Surely Keiko knew more about Asian cooking than Amalia.

"My family has lived in New Mexico for four generations," Keiko continued. Her knife sliced through cilantro in sharp, precise cuts. "My great-grandmother learned to cook from her neighbors—Mexican, Navajo, white ranchers. That fusion, that mixing of traditions, that *is* Southwestern cuisine. But Amalia saw an Asian face and decided I was appropriating. I'm Korean and New Mexican."

"Did you fight back?" Anthone asked. "Refute her review?"

The knife came down harder, thunking into the cutting board. Keiko paused, took a breath, and set it aside.

"The review ran on a Friday. By Monday, we'd lost half our reservations. Within a month, our investor pulled out. Within three months..." She picked up a bunch of sage and started stripping the leaves. "Within three months, my restaurant was gone. My marriage ended six months after that. Turns out financial devastation and public humiliation aren't great for relationships."

She said it with dry humor, but her hands were gripping the herb too tight, crushing the leaves.

"I'm sorry," I said. I thought about what one bad review could do to EB Eats, how fast the Nueva Vida gossip network could turn regulars into ghosts. I could only hope that my friends would stand up for me. "That's a lot to lose."

"That wasn't all." Keiko dropped the mangled sage and reached for fresh sprigs. "I spent about a year trying to drink away the failure. Bartending jobs don't last long when you're sampling the inventory. Ended up in treatment, got clean, stayed clean. Two years of prep cook work in other people's kitchens, saving money, learning to trust myself again."

She gestured to the booth, to the students practicing

their knife work. "This is my first public teaching gig since everything fell apart. Small steps."

I watched her hands move—constant motion that kept her mind busy too. The way she kept checking on her students, protective.

"How did it feel," Kashvi asked, "seeing Amalia here at the festival?"

Keiko's knife slipped, nicking her fingertip. Blood welled up. She grabbed a clean towel, wrapping it without missing a beat. "You want to know if I killed her. That's what this is about."

"We're trying to understand everyone who had history with Amalia," I said.

"Everyone who had motive, you mean." Keiko's laugh was sharp. She looked at each of us. "Yeah, I had motive. Five years ago, I would have cheerfully poisoned her food myself. I fantasized about it during the worst nights—imagining her suffering the way she made me suffer."

One of the students glanced over, and Keiko gave her an encouraging nod before turning back to us.

"But I didn't do it. Because I've spent two years learning that revenge fantasies are just another kind of addiction. They feel good in the moment, but they destroy you from the inside."

"We're asking everyone for their alibi," Anthone said. "Around the time when Amalia died."

"You saw me there." She met my eyes, challenging me to make something of it before turning back to her herbs, resuming her chopping. "I get it. Chef with a destroyed career confronts the critic who ruined her life. It's a neat narrative. But here's what you need to understand—"

She stopped as one of her students called out. "Angle the knife more, Sarah! Yes, like that. Good!"

When she turned back, something in her face had shifted.

"These kids. They're all culinary students from the community college. Half of them are working full-time jobs to afford tuition. They dream about opening restaurants, making something of themselves. And every single one of them will face critics like Amalia, people who can destroy everything they build with a few hundred words."

She gathered the chopped herbs into a bowl.

"I teach them knife skills, but what I'm really teaching them is resilience. How to take criticism without letting it destroy you." She looked up at me. "I can't rebuild my own life if I'm busy destroying someone else's. Even someone who deserved it."

"But you're still angry," Anthone said.

"Of course I'm still angry." Keiko's voice got an edge. "Amalia Limonete was a bully who used her platform to hurt people. She destroyed careers, crushed dreams, and never once showed remorse. The food world is better without her. I swear I didn't kill her."

She grabbed a clean chef's knife and began demonstrating a rock-chop technique to her class. While they began trying to copy her, she whispered to me, "if I killed her, it would have been slower and far more painful."

The words were chilling, made worse by how calm she sounded.

"Keiko—" I started.

"I need to get back to my students. They're paying for a full workshop, and I don't cheat people. That's the difference between me and Amalia. She took everything from people and gave nothing back. I'm trying to give back."

She walked away before we could ask anything else, returning to her students.

"Well," Anthone said as we headed back toward the main festival area. "That was intense."

"She had motive, opportunity, and the knowledge to pull it off," Kashvi said, making notes in her phone. "And that temper..."

"But she's working hard on recovery," I said. "Building a new life."

"Which Amalia's presence threatened," Kashvi pointed out. "Just seeing her critic here might have triggered all those old wounds. Made her feel like she'd never escape."

"She's right about one thing," I said. "If she'd done it, she wouldn't have made it quick. This killing was almost clinical. Efficient. Someone who wanted Amalia dead but didn't need her to suffer."

"Unless that's exactly what she wants us to think," Anthone said.

We walked in silence, the festival sounds washing over us. Somewhere ahead, Rajan held court at his booth. Behind us, Keiko's students were laughing as they practiced their knife work, supervised by a woman who'd lost everything and clawed her way back.

"I don't know if she did it," I admitted. "But I understand why someone might want to."

Kashvi shot me a look. "Does it matter? We all have motives for lots of things, but we don't act on them."

"Maybe. But if we're going to find the truth, we need to understand what pushed someone to murder." I glanced back toward Keiko's booth. "And right now, I'm seeing a lot of people who had very good reasons to want Amalia dead."

14

The *Casita del Sol*'s business center looked like a production studio had exploded across the conference table. Octavia Beaumont had taken over the space with three laptops, their screens showing different angles of festival footage. External hard drives sat among coffee cups and Red Bull cans, cables tangled between devices. I thought how much Alistair would love this opportunity to perform. He'd left town the evening of Amalia's death. Even I couldn't think of him as a suspect, so George let him head out.

Octavia sat in the middle of it all, typing fast. She didn't look up when we walked in, even though the desk clerk had called ahead.

"Ms. Vaughn?" I said. "We need to ask about Amalia Limonete."

"Hang on." She held up one finger, eyes on her screen. "Thirty seconds to save this sequence."

I looked at Kashvi. Most suspects were nervous or defensive. This was new.

The thirty seconds became a full minute before Octavia

glanced up. Early forties, sharp features, red hair in a messy bun. Expensive clothes that looked slept-in. Dark circles under her eyes.

"Sorry." Her tone said she wasn't. "When you're editing, you have to follow the flow." She waved at the chairs across from her. "Sit. This is about Amalia?"

"Yes," I said. "We're questioning everyone who spent time with her during the festival."

"That's me." Octavia turned back to her screen, scrubbing through footage. "We filmed for two full days before she died. Got some great material. Her preparation process was fascinating."

I watched her work a clip of Amalia at her vendor station, arranging bottles. The footage cut mid-sentence, jumping to a different moment that changed the whole context.

"Interesting edit," I said.

Octavia smiled, still focused on her work. "Good television is about finding the story. You just have to know where to cut."

"Even if it changes what someone said?"

"People ramble. They lose their train of thought, circle back, contradict themselves. My job is to make them coherent." She clicked to another sequence. "Watch this."

On screen, Rajan criticized another chef's plating. The clip made him sound arrogant. But I'd been there—he'd praised the same chef's flavors while offering gentle suggestions about technique.

"That's not what he said," Kashvi said.

"It's what he said. I just removed the filler words and the qualifiers. Made it punchy."

"You changed the meaning."

"I revealed the truth beneath the politeness." Octavia

gave us her full attention. "People perform for cameras. They say what they think they should say. My job is to show who they really are."

She believed it. That was the worst part.

"How long have you been producing food shows?" Kashvi asked.

"Fifteen years. Started as a production assistant, worked my way up to producer by twenty-eight." The pride in her voice was hard to miss. "I have a gift for finding good stories and the technical skill to execute them. Three of my shows were nominated for awards."

"Your recent productions haven't done as well," Kashvi said.

Her expression hardened. "The industry's changed. Networks want cheaper content, faster turnarounds. They don't value quality anymore."

"Your last three shows were canceled," I said.

"Because networks panic at the first ratings dip." Her jaw tightened. "They don't give shows time to build audiences. Everything has to be an instant hit, or it's dead."

"So this Amalia Limonete project had to work," Kashvi said.

"It had to be brilliant." Octavia turned to her screens, pulling up more footage. "Amalia was perfect—talented, passionate, with a real story about what makes a success. The show would have been a masterpiece. Could have saved my production company."

She pulled up a shot of Amalia demonstrating tempering, her hands moving with grace. The lighting caught the glossy sheen of melted chocolate.

"Beautiful footage," Kashvi said.

"I know how to shoot food." Octavia adjusted color levels with tiny movements. "I know how to make viewers smell the chocolate through their screens, hear the snap when it breaks. That's craft."

"Then why the manipulative editing?" I asked. "If you're that talented, why not let the truth speak for itself?"

Octavia laughed—bitter and short. "Because truth is boring, Ms. Burton. People don't watch television for truth. They watch for drama, conflict, transformation. They want to see someone triumph or fail. My job is to give them that."

"By destroying people's reputations?" Kashvi's voice had an edge.

"By telling stories." Octavia met her gaze. "If someone's career suffers because they looked arrogant or lazy on camera, maybe they shouldn't have been arrogant or lazy while we were filming."

"Even if you edited out the context?"

"Context doesn't make good television."

I felt sick. She was talking about real people with the same detachment someone might discuss editing stock footage.

"Amalia knew about your editing practices," I said.

Octavia hesitated. "We had discussions about my creative choices."

"Discussions or arguments?"

"She didn't understand the industry. She thought documentary meant objective truth." Octavia's hands stopped moving on her keyboard. "I tried to explain that all documentary is subjective. The moment you choose what to film, how to frame it, what to include—you're creating a narrative."

"But she didn't agree," I said.

"She threatened to go public if I didn't commit to what she called ethical representation." Octavia's laugh was hollow. "As if there's such a thing in television. Everything is performance. As if she was some kind of saint."

"That must have been bad," Kashvi said. "Your whole production company hanging on this show, and your subject threatening to expose your practices."

"She wouldn't have done that." Octavia's confidence came back. "People want what I produce. They don't like it when someone points out how we make the drama. They'll never turn their back on the excitement. And the exposure was too valuable for her business. She was trying to control the narrative."

"And that's your job, right?" Kashvi leaned forward. "What if she planned to expose more than just your editing practices?"

Octavia went pale. "What are you talking about?"

"You tell me." Kashvi kept her voice level. "Did Amalia find something about your past projects? Footage showing more than a little tweak for drama?"

Octavia stared at her screens, footage frozen. Her next words came out much quieter. "Amalia found some raw footage from my previous shows. B-roll that showed differences from the final cuts. Some shady practices I cut out. She said if I didn't agree to her terms, she'd release it to industry publications."

"Ending your career," I said.

"Destroying everything I've built." Octavia's hands clenched. "Fifteen years of work, gone. No network would touch me. My production company would fold. I'd be blacklisted."

Silence except for the laptop fans.

"So you had a problem," Kashvi said. "You needed Amalia alive and cooperative to save your career. But you also needed her silenced to protect it."

"I didn't kill her." Octavia's voice was firm, but her hands shook. "Yes, she had leverage. Yes, I was desperate. But I was trying to negotiate. She was considering my compromise—I'd use a lighter editorial hand if she'd agree not to release the footage."

"Were you reaching an agreement?" I asked.

"We were supposed to meet the morning after the festival. Have a real discussion without the chaos of filming." Octavia closed her laptop screen. "I thought I could convince her that my editing elevated her story. That we could create something brilliant if she'd just trust my vision."

"Where were you during the festival's peak hours?" I asked. "When Amalia was poisoned?"

"Everywhere." Octavia gestured. "That's the problem with being a producer—you're never in one place. I was filming at vendor stations, checking equipment, reviewing footage on my laptop, coordinating with my crew. I walked past Amalia at someone's booth a dozen times."

"Did anyone see you during the tasting event?"

"My cinematographer might have. We were grabbing shots of the crowd. But I also stepped away to review footage, make calls to the network, handle a dozen small crises. There's no way to account for every minute."

Kashvi made a note. "We'll need to talk to your crew."

"Of course." Octavia's professional mask slid back on. "I have nothing to hide."

But she did. Maybe not murder, but plenty of other things.

We left the business center and stood in the hotel lobby.

"She's different from Rajan and Keiko," Kashvi said as we headed to the parking lot. "They were driven by passion

—love or anger or fear. Octavia's drive is professional. Cold. Calculated."

"How did you know about the secret?" I asked. We hadn't found any hints in the documents.

Kashvi put her phone in her pocket and looked around. "If the cops can lie to suspects, why can't we? I knew there was something under all that professional rationalizing."

My phone lit up. *Need you back at the diner. Alf is trying to investigate and has already interrogated three customers.*

I smiled despite everything. "Duty calls."

"Shouldn't we let George know what we've found?" Kashvi asked. "You did promise to share."

Yes, and as usual, that sharing would be one way, with a side of stay out of it. "We don't know anything for sure, yet."

15

Kashvi had to go back to The Open Page, so Jet joined me for the rest of the day. He pulled the van into the small parking lot behind the restaurant at four-thirty.

Maison Delacroix occupied a converted adobe building on the upscale end of Canyon Road. The kind of place with no sign out front because if you had to ask, you couldn't afford it.

"You sure about this timing?" Jet asked. "Won't he be busy?"

"Prep time is perfect," I said. "He'll be working, not performing for customers. And if his son's there, we get both perspectives."

The back entrance led into the kitchen. Stainless steel and tile, each station organized with precision. The air smelled of fresh herbs and something rich reducing on the stove.

Hugo Delacroix stood at the main prep counter, cutting shallots into perfect tiny cubes.

"Mr. Rivers" His voice carried a French accent. "And Ms. Burton. I wondered when you'd come."

"Appreciate you seeing us during prep," I said.

"I'm always working." Hugo swept the shallots into a waiting bowl with the flat of his knife. "Cooking doesn't stop for investigations."

A younger man emerged from the cooler, arms full of vegetables. He turned, and I recognized Amos, Hugo's son.

"Dad?" He set the vegetables down. "Everything okay?"

"It's all fine," Hugo said as he reached for a spoon to taste a sauce.

Amos gave me a look behind his father's back that pleaded for me to keep his secret. Hugo wouldn't appreciate his son's attempt to help me.

"You knew her," I said. "Amalia."

"We had a professional relationship many years ago," Hugo said, returning to his counter. He began separating egg yolks from whites. "It ended poorly. I saw no reason to revisit it."

"We heard you were her protégé," I said. "That she trained you."

"She discovered me, yes." Hugo's tone stayed flat. "I was twenty-three, working in a small bistro in Lyon. She was doing research for her third book. She saw potential."

He set the yolks aside and began whipping the whites.

"She brought me to the States," he continued. "Taught me her approach to creating authenticity in recipes. We worked together for five years, developing new techniques. Wild mushroom preparation—foraging local varieties, preserving their essence. I am ashamed to say I noticed her taking what others created and claiming it for her own. I should have stopped her."

The whites began forming peaks. He never looked at them.

"And then?" Jet asked.

"And then she published her fourth book." Hugo set down the whisk and picked up his knife, working on fresh thyme. "The technique appeared in Chapter seven. Amalia Limonete's Revolutionary Approach to Wild Mushrooms. My name appeared in the acknowledgments. With thanks to Hugo Delacroix for his assistance. I thought we were partners and she treated me like the other chefs she stole from."

"And you ended the relationship," I said.

"Yes. We created it as mentor and protégé," Hugo said, turning his attention to a pile of thyme sprigs. "When she claimed it as her own discovery, there was nothing I could do. Challenging her would have destroyed my career before it began. She was Amalia Limonete. I was nobody."

He swept the thyme into a pile. "So I said nothing. I opened this restaurant, built a reputation, created my own signature dishes. The technique she stole became my calling card anyway—people come here for the mushroom preparations, even if they don't know the real story."

"That must have been difficult," Jet said.

"It was time." Hugo's expression didn't change. "It was a business decision. I chose professional survival over personal vindication."

"But her book was going to tell a different story," I said. "We heard she planned to include something about your work together."

Hugo's hands stilled. He set down the knife.

"She was going to accuse me of theft," he said. "According to her narrative, I stole her technique after she trained me. I stole recipes from young chefs. I had no creativity. Every crime she committed was going to be mine.

She said she was reclaiming her innovation from the protégé who betrayed her trust."

"That's complete bullshit," Amos said. "She was the thief. Everyone who knows my father knows he's the one who developed that method. But her book would have made him look like—"

"Amos." Hugo's voice cut through. "Please check the temperature on the duck confit."

Amos opened his mouth, then closed it and moved to the other side of the kitchen.

"Your son seems protective," Jet said.

"He knows the full story." Hugo started on a fennel bulb. "He knows what I sacrificed to build this restaurant, and how fragile reputation is in this industry. He knows that Amalia's book could have destroyed everything."

"So you had motive," Jet said.

"Yes, I had reason to kill her." Hugo kept working. "My restaurant would have suffered. My reputation would have been questioned. After thirty years of building something real, I would have been reduced to a footnote in Amalia's narrative of betrayal."

He set down the knife and met Jet's eyes. His gaze didn't waver.

"But if I had killed her, the book would still exist in draft form. It would still come out, probably with even more sympathy for her position. Killing her wouldn't erase the accusation. It would only make it permanent."

"Unless you destroyed the manuscript," I said.

"Which I didn't do." Hugo turned to his stove, adding the shallots to a heated pan. They sizzled.

"You seem calm about all this," I said. "Discussing someone who betrayed you, who was about to ruin your reputation."

Hugo didn't speak while he adjusted the heat.

"I stopped feeling things about Amalia a long time ago," he said. "She taught me that emotional investment in professional relationships is a weakness. I learned that lesson well."

"Maybe too well," Amos muttered.

Hugo glanced at his son. For a second, something flickered across his face—not warmth, but an acknowledgment of connection.

"My son thinks I'm too controlled," Hugo said. "He may be right. But control has served me better than passion ever did. Amalia proved that."

He plated a small portion of his reduction, adding vegetables and a sprig of thyme. The presentation was beautiful, balanced, finessed.

"This is what I built," he said, gesturing to the kitchen. "A restaurant with a two-month waiting list. A James Beard nomination. A reputation built on my own innovation, not borrowed glory. Amalia's book could have damaged that, yes. But killing her would have been worse. It would have been... inelegant."

The word hung in the air.

"Thank you for your time," I said. "Have the police been here already?" It occurred to me it would be good to know the progress of the official investigation.

"I was under the impression that you didn't worry about the real investigators." Hugo said. "Now I must ask you to leave. Cooking doesn't stop."

We sat in Jet's van thinking about what we'd learned. At least I did. Jet didn't say anything.

"He's right—killing her doesn't erase the manuscript. It might even make its publication more likely, more sympathetic to her version." I watched a car pull into the lot. "And something about the way he talked about her... it was like discussing a technique that didn't work out. Clinical. Detached."

"Detached enough to plan a poisoning?"

"Maybe. Or detached because he learned to survive betrayal by feeling nothing."

"He's hiding something, maybe more trauma than he cares to admit," Jet said. "Or guilt."

"Could be either." I buckled my seatbelt. "What about Amos?"

"Protective of his father." Jet started the engine. "Could see him trying to save his dad from that book's damage. Maybe he came by the bookstore to find out what we knew?"

"You know what bothers me most?" I said. "Hugo was a victim. Amalia really did steal his work, take credit for something they created together. And then she would make him the villain in her story. But the victim might have become the perpetrator."

"And she accused Octavia of enhancing the drama." Jet took the turn toward town.

Hypocrisy isn't a crime.

16

Click-click-click. The camera shutter sound pulled my attention to the Open Page's front window. Through the glass, I saw Birdie Castellanos crouched beside one of Kashvi's bistro tables, phone angled at a cappuccino.

"Hold on," she said to someone off-screen—her phone propped on a stack of books, filming. "The light's not quite right."

I pushed open the door, Kashvi and Jet behind me. The bell chimed, but Birdie didn't look up. She adjusted the cup's position, tilted it, checked the screen, adjusted again.

"Just a second," she said, still focused on the cup. Then her whole demeanor shifted. Her face brightened, her voice jumped an octave. "Hey friends! Birdie here, coming to you from the Open Page Bookstore in Nueva Vida. Can we just take a moment to appreciate this cappuccino art? The barista next door is talented."

She held the cup to the camera, turning it to catch the light. The foam art was impressive—a perfect leaf pattern.

"And the best part? This place has the most incredible

reading nook energy. Like, I could spend all day here with a good book and endless coffee." She took a sip, smiled at the camera. "Okay, not sponsored, but if you're ever in New Mexico, this is a must-visit. Link to their Instagram in my stories!"

She tapped her screen, and the bright energy drained from her face. She slumped back in her chair, looking exhausted.

"I'm impressed," Kashvi said. Birdie's head snapped up, eyes widening.

This was too good an opportunity to let pass. "We'd like to talk, if you have time," I said.

Birdie glanced at her phone, checking something—probably her follower count or engagement metrics. "Yeah. Of course. About Amalia Limonete, right?" She tapped the screen, posting the video. "Can I buy you coffee? The lavender oat milk latte is amazing."

"We're fine," I said, settling into one of the mismatched chairs. The bookstore was quiet this afternoon—just a couple students in the far corner with their laptops. Jazz played from hidden speakers, and the whole space smelled comfortingly of old books.

Birdie set her phone face-down on the table but kept glancing at it.

"You were at the festival yesterday morning," Kashvi said. "During the tasting event."

"Yeah, I was documenting everything for my platforms." Birdie picked up her phone, scrolled. "Instagram stories, TikTok, my blog. I posted forty-seven times from yesterday alone."

"That's a lot of content," Jet said.

"That's the job." Birdie's voice had an edge. "People think it's just taking pretty pictures of food, but it's constant work.

Filming, editing, engaging with comments, maintaining the algorithm, collaborating with brands. I post at least four times a day across all platforms."

I thought about the bright, enthusiastic person she'd been on camera versus the tired woman sitting across from me. "Must be exhausting."

Relief flickered across Birdie's face. "It is. But it's how you build a following. Consistency, authenticity, engagement. My audience expects a certain energy from me."

"Authenticity?" I said. The woman who posted clips was definitely not the real version.

Birdie's jaw tightened. "I know what you're thinking. That it's all fake, all performance. That's what Amalia thought."

"What did Amalia say to you?" I asked.

Birdie's phone vibrated. She glanced at it, then looked away. "She said I was part of what's ruining food culture. That social media influencers are all fake and manufactured expertise. Those were her exact words. She said people like me are convincing audiences we're experts when we're just pretty faces who know how to work an algorithm."

"That must have hurt," Kashvi said.

"The thing is, I do know about food." Birdie's voice rose. "I've worked in restaurants since I was sixteen. I've staged at some incredible kitchens in Phoenix—did a three-month unpaid internship at Barrio Café learning from Chef Silvana Salcido Esparza. I've taken sommelier courses, studied bread-making with a master baker, traveled to Oaxaca to learn traditional mole from local cooks."

She pulled out her phone, started scrolling, showing us photos that weren't the polished Instagram posts. These were behind-the-scenes shots—Birdie in kitchen whites covered in flour, taking notes while watching a chef work, sitting with elderly women in Mexico who were teaching her to grind spices.

"I do the work," she said. "But when I post on Instagram, I don't lead with my credentials because that's not what my audience wants. They want someone relatable, accessible. Someone who makes them feel like discovering great food is something they can do too, not some exclusive thing that requires a culinary degree."

I studied the photos.

"Were you one of the influencers she was focusing on for her article?" Jet asked.

"She wouldn't say, but yeah. I could tell." Birdie twisted one of her bracelets. "She kept asking me questions about my background, my training, how I research my posts. It felt like an interrogation."

"An article like that could damage your career," Kashvi said.

"You have to understand—my entire income depends on brand partnerships and affiliate marketing. Companies pay me because I have an engaged following that trusts my recommendations. If Amalia published something that made me look like a fraud, like I've been lying to my audience about my expertise, that trust disappears overnight."

"Have you been lying?" Kashvi asked.

"No. But I've been strategic." Birdie picked up her cappuccino and took a sip. "I don't hide my training, but I don't lead with it either. I present myself as an enthusiastic food lover who wants to share great discoveries, not as a formally trained chef who's judging from on high. That's a deliberate choice because it's what works on social media. It's what makes people feel connected to me instead of intimidated."

"So you're knowledgeable, but you present yourself as

learning along with your audience," I said. That wasn't a motive for murder.

"Exactly. And Amalia was going to frame that as deception." Birdie's frustration built. "The enthusiasm is real, it's just that I also happen to have formal training backing up my instincts."

Her phone buzzed again. This time she didn't glance at it.

"The world is changing," Birdie said. "Food criticism used to be these elite gatekeepers at major newspapers deciding what was worth eating. Now it's democratized—anyone with a phone and a palate can build an audience and share recommendations. Amalia hated that. She hated that someone like me could have more influence than critics with journalism degrees and decades of experience."

"Did she have a point about standards?" Jet asked. "About the difference between trained expertise and popular opinion?"

"Maybe. But maybe her way wasn't the only right way either." Birdie met Jet's eyes. "I've had people tell me I helped them discover restaurants they never would have tried otherwise. My followers trust me because I'm not some elitist critic—I'm eating the same meals they can afford, shopping at the same markets they shop at."

I thought about EB Eats, about how most of my customers found me through word of mouth and social media posts, not restaurant reviews. "There's value in that kind of promotion."

"Amalia didn't think so. She said I was lowering standards, making people think opinion is the same as expertise." Birdie's voice wavered. "And maybe that's true for some influencers. But not all of us. Not me."

"Where were you when the event was happening?" I asked.

"Filming." Birdie pulled up her phone, started showing us her Instagram stories from the previous day. "I documented the whole morning—different vendor booths, interviews with chefs, behind-the-scenes prep work. I've got exact timestamps for everything."

I watched her scroll. It was an impressive record. Birdie at 9:47 AM filming a tortilla-making demonstration. Birdie at 10:15 AM interviewing a salsa vendor about her family recipe. Birdie at 10:52 AM capturing the setup of the main tasting tent.

"Someone poisoned Amalia with cyanide," I said. "That required planning—knowing how to get the poison, understanding how to mask the taste, having access to her food at exactly the right moment. It's not something you could do on impulse."

Birdie's eyes widened. "You think I—because I'm good at planning content, you think I planned a murder?"

"We're just trying to understand who had the capability and the motive," Kashvi said gently.

"I document everything I do for social media." Birdie's voice rose. "That's the opposite of what you'd want if you were planning to kill someone. I put my location, my activities, my whole life online constantly."

"Unless that's the perfect cover," Jet said. "Being so visible that no one suspects you could have time to do something hidden."

Birdie stood, her bracelets jingling. "This is insane. I wanted Amalia to leave me alone, not—I would never—" She pressed her palms against her eyes. "God, do you know what would happen to my career if people thought I was a murder suspect?"

Her phone buzzed again. She grabbed it, looked at the screen, and I saw distress cross her face. "I have to respond to this. I have a sponsored post going live in twenty minutes and the brand wants approval on the caption."

We were discussing murder, and she had to approve social media captions.

"I didn't kill Amalia," Birdie said, typing on her phone, not looking at us. "I'm not sorry she's gone, because honestly? The world is better off without critics who think the only valid way to appreciate food is their way. But I didn't kill her."

She finished typing, hit send, then turned it off. "I'm not like Amalia I understand resilience. She thought you needed institutions and credentials to have authority. I know you just need passion and persistence. She could have written whatever she wanted about me—I would have survived it."

"Then why were you so worried about it?" Kashvi asked.

"Because survival and thriving aren't the same thing." Birdie's voice dropped. "Because I grew up being invisible, being told I wasn't smart enough or serious enough, being dismissed as just the pretty middle child who wants attention. And I built something where people pay attention to what I have to say. Where my opinion matters. Amalia planned to take that away and make me invisible again."

"But you just said you could rebuild," Jet pointed out.

"I could. Doesn't mean I wanted to." Birdie grabbed her cappuccino, grimaced at it. "Look, I'm not going to pretend I'm some mature person who rises above criticism. I'm twenty-nine, I struggle with impostor syndrome constantly, and half the time I'm terrified that everyone will realize I have no idea what I'm doing. Amalia threatening to expose me as a fraud? Even though I'm not one? That was my nightmare."

"Someone killed her. Was your nightmare enough?" I asked.

Birdie met my eyes. "No. Because at the end of the day, I love food. I love discovering new restaurants, learning about different cuisines, helping people find places that serve incredible meals. That's real. That matters. And no article, no matter how mean, could take away the fact that I know what good food tastes like and I'm helping people find it."

She stood, gathering her phone and her bag. "I need to go film my lunch content before it's too late in the day. But I'll tell you this—Amalia's whole approach to food criticism was about gate-keeping. About deciding who deserved to have a voice and who didn't. The world is better with more voices, not fewer. Even if those voices use Instagram instead of newspaper columns."

After she left, the three of us sat thinking for a moment.

"Well," Jet said. "That was different from our other suspect interviews."

"Different generation, different medium, different values," Kashvi said. "But the same underlying theme—Amalia threatened something important to her."

"She's right that the world is changing," I said. "Food criticism doesn't just belong to newspaper critics anymore. But Amalia was also right that expertise matters, that there's value in training and credentials."

"Both things can be true," Kashvi said. "And Birdie's caught in the middle—knowledgeable but presenting herself as just an enthusiastic amateur because that's what works algorithmically."

"Question is," Jet said, "do we believe her?"

"She has the capability," I said. "The knowledge, the

access, the understanding of planning and timing. I guess anyone could get what they needed with a search. Her motive is the weakest."

"But is she ruthless enough?" Kashvi asked. "That's what I can't figure out."

"Desperation can make people ruthless," Jet said. "Especially when it's not just about career, but about identity. About finally being seen and validated after a lifetime of being invisible."

"Add her to the list," I said. "Not the strongest motive, but definite capability, and enough knowledge of food science and research to figure out how to poison someone."

Kashvi wrote in her notebook. "We're building quite a collection of people who wanted Amalia gone."

"Yeah," I said, standing. "Now we need to figure out which one of them wanted her dead badly enough to actually do it."

My phone announced a text: Anthone. *Afternoon rush starting early. Could use you at the diner.*

Real life, pulling me back from the murder investigation to the daily rhythm of running a restaurant.

17

Felix Kowalski's warehouse sat on the industrial edge of Nueva Vida, where the town's charm ended and the work got done. The building had thick adobe walls that predated most of the restaurants it supplied, wooden loading doors smoothed by decades of use, and hand-painted signs advertising "Kowalski Specialty Foods - Serving the Southwest Since 1947."

Jet and I pulled up as Felix climbed out of a delivery truck, clipboard in hand. He looked tired in a bone-deep way.

"Mr. Kowalski?" Jet called out. "We appreciate you making time to talk with us."

Felix set down his clipboard. "Had a feeling you'd get around to me. Everyone knows Amalia helped destroy my family's business once. Guess people assume I'd want revenge. I told the cops everything, but everyone knows you're on the case too." No bitterness in his voice, just resignation. "Come on. I'm doing inventory anyway—might as well talk while I work."

The warehouse smelled of cumin and dried chilies,

coffee beans and imported olive oil. Industrial shelving stretched toward exposed wooden beams, organized with the care that came from generations of practice. Near the office, black-and-white photographs lined the wall—the same building in the 1940s, a younger version in the 1960s, always with Kowalski family members standing beside delivery trucks.

"My grandfather started this business after the war," Felix said, following my gaze. "Imported specialty ingredients nobody else in the region could get. Built relationships with vendors in Mexico, Spain, Italy. We were the place restaurants called when they needed something specific, something authentic."

He moved to a section of shelving, checking items against his inventory sheet. The work seemed to steady him.

"That's impressive," I said. "Three generations is rare these days."

"Almost four." Felix's hand paused over a box of imported peppercorns. "My daughter was supposed to take over after me. She was getting her business degree, learning the operation summers and weekends. Then the contamination incident happened."

Jet pulled out his notebook. "That was seven years ago?"

"Seven years, four months, and sixteen days." Felix marked something on his clipboard. "We'd been working with a new supplier out of El Paso. They sent us a batch of ground cumin that looked fine, smelled fine, passed our normal quality checks. But there was contamination in the processing facility—not our fault, nothing we could have caught without laboratory testing."

"Amalia's investigation exposed that?" I asked.

"More than exposed it. She traced every restaurant that had used our cumin, tested dishes, published findings that made it sound like we were running some kind of negligent operation." Felix moved to the next shelf section. "The contamination was real—I'm not saying it wasn't. Three people got sick, though nobody was seriously hurt. We recalled everything, cooperated with health inspectors."

He paused, looking at the photographs. "But the way Amalia wrote about it... she didn't just report the problem. She questioned our entire quality control system, implied we'd been cutting corners for years. Suddenly restaurants that had trusted us for decades were canceling contracts. Our reputation, built over seventy years, was gone in a month."

"That must have been devastating," I said.

"My father had a stroke two months after her article came out. Stress, the doctors said. He'd spent forty years building on what his father started, and he watched it collapse." Felix's voice roughened. "He died thinking he'd failed the family legacy. My daughter changed her major, went into nursing instead. Didn't want anything to do with the business."

George made notes. "You rebuilt though. The business is still operating."

"Barely." Felix gestured around the warehouse. "We're a fraction of what we were. I had to let go of employees who'd been with us for twenty years. Now it's just me and two part-timers. We lost all our high-end restaurant accounts. Most of what we do now is basic supply for smaller establishments, festival vendors, catering services."

"Including vendors at the latest event?" I asked.

"That's right. I supplied ingredients to about half the vendors there. That Limonete woman ordered a specialty product while she was in town." Felix's laugh held nothing. "She needed Mexican vanilla and cinnamon from Veracruz.

I'm one of the few suppliers who can still get it. Business is business, I guess."

The admission sharpened my attention. "So you had access to her supplies?"

"I had access to everyone's supplies. That's the nature of the work." Felix looked at me. "I delivered orders to the grounds the day before the event started. Multiple trips, and I wasn't the only vendor. Nobody pays attention to the supply guy—I'm background noise while chefs are doing their prep work."

Jet shifted. "Did you see or talk with Amalia during those deliveries?"

"Briefly. She checked her order, thanked me, that was it." Felix returned to his inventory, checking expiration dates on spice containers. "She was polite, actually. Always was, even after she destroyed my family's business. That's the thing about Amalia—I don't think she ever meant to be cruel. She just believed in her mission so much that she didn't consider the collateral damage."

"Has there been another investigation?" I asked.

Felix's shoulders tensed. "The state health department has been asking questions about our import documentation. Nothing formal yet, but the inspector who came by last month had copies of Amalia's recent research. She'd been looking into specialty food suppliers again, questioning whether smaller operations like mine meet the same standards as larger distributors."

"Was she right to question that?" I asked.

"I don't know." He looked pained. "My documentation is thorough, but some suppliers work on relationships and trust rather than paperwork. Modern regulations don't care about trust or tradition." He gestured around the warehouse. "This is all I have left. My father's legacy, my grandfather's dream. If another scandal hits, we won't recover."

The words echoed in the warehouse, bouncing off shelves stocked with ingredients that connected Nueva Vida's restaurants to traditions spanning continents and generations.

Jet looked around at the full warehouse. "That's a dangerous position to be in."

"Is it?" Felix looked between us. "Or is it liberating? When you've already lost everything that mattered what's one more loss?" He set down his clipboard. "I was angry when Amalia died. Not because I killed her, but because I realized I was relieved. Relieved that she couldn't finish destroying what little I'd managed to rebuild."

The honesty was startling. Either he was innocent or he was the best liar I'd met yet.

"Where were you during the event?" Jet asked.

"Making deliveries to three different festival vendors. I have invoices, timestamps, vendor signatures." Felix moved to his office area, pulling files from an organized cabinet. "I was working, same as always. Trying to keep this place running one delivery at a time."

I looked at the photographs again—generations of Kowalskis standing beside their business, not knowing that one contamination incident and one critic's investigation would nearly end what war, depression, and changing times hadn't.

"Did Amalia know?" I asked. "About your father? About your daughter abandoning the business?"

Felix paused. "I wrote that woman a letter, about six months after her article. Told her what had happened to my family. Asked her if she thought the public good was worth that cost."

"Did she respond?"

"She did. She said she was sorry for our pain, but that protecting consumers had to take priority over protecting business interests. She said she hoped we'd recover, but that she couldn't regret exposing a genuine safety issue."

"How did that make you feel?" I asked.

"Like she was both right and wrong at the same time." Felix returned the letter to its folder. "People could have been seriously hurt. She did serve the public good by exposing it. But did she have to go so far?"

Jet closed his notebook. "Thanks for talking to us, Mr. Kowalski. You didn't have to tell us anything."

"Honesty is all I can offer." Felix walked us toward the warehouse entrance, past shelves of organized ingredients. "You out-investigated those two detectives before. Please do it again soon."

The afternoon sun cast long shadows across the industrial lot. I glanced back at the warehouse, seeing generations in those thick adobe walls.

"He had the most opportunity," I said as we reached the car. "And opportunity. Access to supplies."

"And the most complex motive," Jet added. "Not just revenge for the past but bringing an end to a new campaign by Amalia."

I wasn't sure her death would stop the new investigation, but without her prodding them, perhaps the inspectors would be more reasonable. "Does that make him more or less likely to be our killer?"

Jet started the van, but didn't put it in gear. "None of the people we talked to seem like they'd kill. That's the problem, right? We have a list of people and the killer should be on it, but no one is standing out."

The Open Page had closed early for our war council. Will and Jacquie were happy to keep the diner going so I could focus on getting somewhere with our investigation. Anthone switched his apron for a hoodie and joined me for the short walk.

I'd send a text to George because I figured he'd hear about us talking to suspects. All I said was, we haven't found anything you don't probably know.

He'd texted back: *be careful. Don't eat or drink anything.*

Kashvi had rearranged her back room and the special wallpaper that we could write on like a whiteboard was already cluttered with sticky notes and printouts.

Jet and I shared what we knew. Kashvi and Anthone took turns adding new notes to the wall. By the time we finished talking the wall looked like someone had shaken up a Mondrian painting.

"Okay," Kashvi said, stepping up to the board. "Time to organize? Or do we add the gossip first?"

I still held onto a nagging feeling we were missing someone. Jet was right. We had a list of likely suspects and yet none of them seemed like they'd kill Amalia for any motive. "Gossip. We need more names. I'm not sure our attempt at being more professional is working. Our success has always been because of a rumor."

"Yeah, I liked it better before," Kashvi said. "This time I feel like I'm being stuck outside the fun."

"If we get this all organized, maybe we'll be back to the fun part," Jet said. "What's the gossip?"

Kashvi grabbed her notebook. Way at the first case we solved, she'd provided us with one each to keep our notes in. She'd insisted on a new book for each case. The cover of mine was a fat tuxedo cat glaring out with My tuna is more important than your coffee written over it. Not quite Macchiato's breed, but certainly her attitude.

"Okay. Amalia was not well liked by anyone. Mrs. Waverly said she was sure the nice comments were an act. The way she treated her nephew was reprehensible. That came with a different word, but I cleaned it up."

I wrote Knox's name on a sticky note. "He seemed devoted to her."

"Maybe he learned from Amalia how to pretend," Anthone said. "He was everywhere with her. Lots of opportunity, just like everyone else."

"But no motive," Jet said. "We need details."

I added an item to our action list: talk to Mrs. Waverly.

"We haven't really talked to Knox," Kashvi said. "Add that."

I complied. "If feels like we're back to familiar territory. Gossip then suspect."

We stood looking at the notes trying to see some connections. "Any other tidbits?"

Kashvi took a note and wrote Cleo's name. "I haven't heard any gossip, but adding Knox to the list made me wonder why we haven't considered her."

That was an excellent point. When had we decided to exclude names from our suspect list? Was it because Cleo seemed so distraught, or that she helped us? And I hadn't even questioned Knox's reaction.

18

The third pot of coffee was brewing when Cleo Fontaine walked into The Open Page at ten the next morning. She looked exhausted. We all did.

"Thank you for coming," I said, gesturing to the empty chair at our table. "I know this isn't easy."

"Easy doesn't cover it." Cleo set down a leather portfolio I recognized from the festival. "But if what I know helps find who did this, then talking about Amalia's quirks feels necessary."

Anthone brought her coffee without asking—black with one sugar, the way we'd seen her drink it at the festival.

"The police asked about her schedule, her business dealings," Cleo said. "Nobody asked about her as a person. The things that made her who she was."

"That's what we're looking for," Kashvi said. "The personal details. Things only someone close would know."

Cleo opened her portfolio. Meticulous notes in precise handwriting filled the pages. "Amalia was terrified of bees. Not just allergic—phobic. She'd walk three blocks out of her way to avoid a hive. Same with spiders. She once made me cancel a restaurant inspection because there was a web near the entrance."

I glanced at Jet, who was adding this to our notes. "What about dietary restrictions?"

"Beyond what she'd admit in print?" Cleo's laugh was hollow. "She was lactose intolerant but would never acknowledge it in reviews. Said it made her look weak. She took enzyme pills before every meal—kept them in a silver case in her purse, and she couldn't stand sweetness. Her palate was refined for bitterness, but actual sugar overwhelmed her."

"The dark chocolate mousse," I said. "That's why she looked so happy to see it for judging."

"Right. She struggled with desserts at every contest. I think she tried to be fair, but it didn't often come across that way."

Kashvi looked up from her notebook. "How many people knew that she didn't like too much sweet?"

"Knox did. He'd photographed her at dozens of events. Hugo probably—he worked with her for two years. But the general public? They just saw her eating dessert."

I wished I could just write this on our murder wall, but we didn't want any of our suspects knowing what we'd learned. "Let's put opportunity and motive aside for now. We need to think about this more personally. Who knew her habits? The killer didn't need to take advantage of a chance, they could just manufacture one."

"They needed to know her preferences," Anthone added. "What flavors she'd accept, what she'd reject. Maybe even how she'd do the tasting. Her own spoon or supplied implements?"

"Let's go through our suspects," I said making sure we wouldn't include Cleo in that list. "Rajan Okoye had motive, but did he know Amalia personally? Enough to do what he needed to so she'd take the poison."

"He might," Cleo said. "It was a long time ago, but Amalia didn't change her habits easily."

"Octavia Beaumont," Kashvi said. "Was it just a professional relationship?"

Cleo shook her head. "All business. Contracts and publication schedules. She wouldn't know about the her phobias, the intolerance, the dark chocolate, any of it."

In my head the lines on our murder wall were shifting and starting to form something like a pattern.

"Birdie Castellanos," I said. "She wanted Amalia to review do a live stream with her, but had they met before the event."

"Never," Cleo confirmed. "Amalia mentioned her in notes once. Not convinced it is a good idea. That's it."

"Keiko Nakamura?" Jet's asked.

"Professional only," Cleo said. "Keiko would know how Amalia wanted food presented, not how she ate in private. Not her health issues or fears."

"Felix Kowalski," Anthone said. "He supplied her kitchen."

"Felix knew what ingredients she ordered," Cleo agreed. "Not why. Not her personal preferences. Just orders to fill."

Pretty much all our list crossed out. My mental picture of the murder board went blank. I wasn't exactly happy we were right about everyone we'd interviewed. They didn't know who Amalia Limonete was as a person.

"That leaves three people," Kashvi said. "Knox Thorne, Amos Delacroix, and you, Cleo."

Cleo didn't flinch. "I know. I thought about it all night. We're the only ones who knew her well enough. Knox grew up around her and worked with her at all her events. Amos is really angry about how she treated his dad. But he had hardly any contact with her. And I worked with her every day for three years. Knox and I knew everything about her. I didn't kill her and I can't believe Knox would have done it."

I wanted to believe her, but a killer would lie and well. I wanted Cleo to leave so we could go back to the murder wall and bring this new information together but there were a few questions we needed answers for.

"Does Knox have a motive?" I asked still trying to think about how I could ask Cleo for hers.

"I'm not supposed to know this, but..." She pulled up something on her phone but didn't show us. "There was a family trust that Amalia wanted to control. Knox said he didn't care as long as he got his payment as usual. I don't think I believed him, or maybe I expected Amalia to cut him off if she could."

"She'd do that?" Jet asked.

"She was always saying little things about standing on your own two feet, to him." Cleo put her phone down. "Now I think about it more, I think that's exactly what she was planning to do. Cut off all the people getting payments."

A powerful motive. I glanced at Jet and Kashvi to see if they thought the same. A quick nod told me they agreed.

"And your motive?" Anthone asked saving me the trouble.

Cleo nodded. "I had means, motive, opportunity, and knowledge. I understand why I'm on the suspect list. I don't have a motive. Working for her was hard, but going to any other critic would be a step down at best. I'm not like Birdie.

I can't build a brand. Amalia was my brand. Now she's gone, I don't know what to do."

Everything about her was screaming despair and fear. She was telling the truth and I couldn't find any trace of doubt in my head. Cleo didn't do this. "You should get some rest," I said. "I'm sure something will come up. We'll figure this out."

She picked up her phone and dropped it in her bag. "Maybe I'll dream about a new job. Or not. You're right. I need sleep more than anything else."

When she was gone, Mallory, Kashvi's part-time helper, took over the bookstore, and we headed into the back room. It was crowded with Anthone joining us, but we didn't need space, we needed privacy.

"Okay, let's clean the board up now we have new information." I stepped forward but Jet nudged me back.

"I'll do it. And I'll add what we know." He swept every sticky note and red thread to the floor before wiping the marker off. "Suspects?"

"We can't just put Knox up there," I said. "Add Cleo and Amos. Even if we eliminate them, we need to avoid focusing on one person.

"Knox has a chemistry background," Kashvi said, checking her notes. "His degree before he went into photography. Amos might not know Amalia well enough, but who knows what his dad told him."

"Cleo could have been acting," Anthone said. "I bought her whole poor me I'm lost without her thing, but we don't know her."

Jet wrote the names and motives for each person on the board. I liked that it looked so simple, but still no real connection.

"We need to focus on how the poison was delivered," I said. "Everyone had the opportunity, all three have motives."

"We started with too many suspects," Kashvi said. "Now we have too few, and they all feel possible."

"We should have been investigating two of them from the start," I said. "The ones she trusted. The ones who had access to her life. Amos is the weakest suspect. Knox and Cleo are more likely."

19

The morning rush had died down when Knox walked in, camera bag over one shoulder, dark circles under his eyes. I waved him to the counter where Jet was refilling the coffee station. Lissa and Lola managed the remaining diners, and Jacquie's shift was starting soon.

"You look rough," I said, reaching for a mug. I'd sent Knox a text earlier to ask him to join me here at EB EATS. We'd all decided that confronting him here was a much safer option than the kind we'd done in the past.

"Coffee. Please." He dropped onto a stool and set his camera bag by his feet. "Can't stop seeing her at that table. Every time I close my eyes."

I poured and slid the cup across. "When did you eat last?"

"Yesterday morning, I think. I tried to eat dinner, but I couldn't get anything down."

"Let me get you some chili and cornbread."

He nodded, and I headed to the kitchen to ladle up a

bowl from the pot Anthone had started that morning. When I came back, Knox was staring into his coffee.

"She wasn't supposed to be the scary food critic," he said. "When I was a kid, she was just Aunt Amalia. Took me to galleries and museums, told me about photographers who changed the world. She gave me my first real camera for my fourteenth birthday."

I set the bowl in front of him. "It was kind of her to help you find your path."

"She said every photographer should start with something that makes you slow down and think about each shot." His mouth almost curved into a smile. "Spent a whole weekend teaching me how to use it. Then she hired me. Although I guess that's not the right word. Aunt Amalia didn't pay me. She said I had enough from the trust fund. Working with her was reward enough."

I heard bitterness in his tone, but his expression didn't match. A sadness in his eyes as if he regretted losing his lovely aunt to the hard woman she became.

"She used to be softer. When I moved to Santa Fe to do photography full-time, she had me over for dinner every Sunday. Nothing fancy, just the two of us. She'd make this incredible *coq au vin* and we'd talk about art, about finding your voice. She got what it was like to try making something that mattered in a world that mostly doesn't care."

And now he was our number one suspect in her murder. "What changed?"

Knox took a bite of stew, chewed and swallowed with difficulty. "Time. Success. She got harder over the years. Brittle. Like she was defending territory all the time, waiting for the next attack. I tried to get her to talk about it, but she'd just change the subject. Say she was fine, that criticism was lonely but someone had to do it right."

The door opened, Kashvi walked in followed by Cleo. The sleep hadn't helped her. Cleo looked worse than Knox, her usual polished appearance gone to pieces.

"Thought I might find you here," Cleo said to Knox. She glanced at me. "Somewhere we can talk? All of us?"

I led them to the back booth where we'd been running our investigation. Jet brought over coffee and a fresh pot.

"I've been thinking about what you said," Cleo said, her voice thick with exhaustion. "I worked with her three years, and I saw things. Moments when the armor cracked."

"Like what?" Kashvi picked up her mug.

"Late nights at the office, after everyone else left. I'd hear her in her office. Crying." Cleo's hands shook around her mug. "Once I knocked, asked if she was okay. She wiped her eyes and said, not to be so intrusive. She didn't like people seeing her vulnerable."

"I don't think she liked being vulnerable," Knox said. "Some of the things she did made me wonder if she enjoyed hurting people. Destroying careers."

Cleo nodded. "She stopped taking protégés before I came along."

"Yeah, she said they all betrayed her in the end," Knox said. "But... never mind it's not important."

He was lying. "But what?" I asked. "Details might help."

Knox looked away and took a deep breath like he was grabbing some courage. "You're not supposed to speak ill of the dead."

"If you know something that explains why someone would murder your aunt, you need to speak up," Kashvi said. "It's not like people thought she was a saint."

"It's not something I can prove," he said, still hedging.

Why was he avoiding the answer? Was it really about

preserving some image he had of her, or had he not meant to speak that word, but.

"You're right. She says they all betrayed her, but it didn't look like that to me." He poked at the chili again. "She started out with all of them in a good place. They needed her mentorship, she needed their admiration. Then when any of her projects started getting ideas of their own, she turned on them."

Cleo leaned forward. "So the facts weren't true?"

"They were," he said. "But I suspect she set everything up. Gave them some encouragement to be creative, to not worry so much about convention. Then she'd swoop in when someone crossed a line."

Cleo sat back suddenly. "That would explain a lot. I always though she just had bad taste in chefs."

"I noticed she was getting worse—harder." Knox's voice cracked. "I though it was stress. I suggested she take a break, maybe write a book about the good side of food instead of just reviews. She'd laugh and say, that's not who I am anymore, Knox. This is what I'm good at."

"Did she have anyone else? Besides you?" I asked. If I could get him talking long enough, maybe he'd say something that supported my feeling that he wasn't telling the whole truth, or something that would clear him.

"Not really. My father—her brother—died five years ago. Heart attack." Knox rubbed his face. "That made it worse. He left the family trust in mom's hands. Amalia didn't like that. I tried to stay away from the topic, but I know she was pushing to take control."

Cleo pulled out her phone and scrolled. "She sent me a text last month. I didn't think it was important at the time, but now..." She turned the screen toward us. "It said, you should be looking for another employer. I have taught you all I know. She fired me at least once a week, and I thought this was the same thing."

Why did Cleo stay? I would have walked out the first time she fired me. Was it so she could poison Amalia? Between the two suspects in the booth, both were giving me the feeling they were the killer.

Knox shook his head. "She was still fighting. Still planning her next review, her next piece. But she was tired. Told me something big was in the works."

"I don't know about any big plans," Cleo said. "From what I saw, she was getting ready to tear a lot of people down, but in the usual way."

"If one of her victims found out... Cyanide poisoning requires proximity," I said. "It requires knowledge. And it requires cold calculation. Whoever killed your aunt knew her well enough to hate her enough to set this up."

"Or love her enough to want her silenced," Kashvi said.

Knox grabbed his camera bag. "If someone I know killed Aunt Amalia, if someone who sat at her table and smiled at her did this... I need to know. She was impossible and cruel and lonely, but she was family. She deserved better."

He didn't look me in the eye as he spoke. I know there could be a million reasons why, but all I felt was lies.

Knox headed back out into the bright New Mexico morning, Cleo following behind. I watched him go. We didn't need to interview him. Something in his denial rang false. His casual dismissal of Amalia's attempt to control the family trust. The quiet way he tried to make her look like a loving aunt.

If he thought I suspected him, this would get dangerous.

Kashvi turned from watching him leave. "Next step?"

"Time to call George," I said. "I'm pretty sure he hasn't heard Knox talk about his aunt that way."

20

"We announce we found her notebook," Kashvi said, tapping the center of the board. "That we know who killed her."

"Even though we don't actually have it," Jet added. He leaned against the bookshelf, arms crossed.

I nodded, feeling the weight of what we were proposing. "I don't see any other way to force the killer to reveal themselves. We leak that we're meeting tomorrow afternoon to discuss what's in it. Make it sound like we're deciding whether to go to the police or handle it privately."

"Bait," Vic said from his position near the window. He'd been quiet since we started, watching and listening. "You're making yourselves targets. I need to be there."

"To protect me?" I didn't need Vic getting on that bandwagon. George was going to fight us on this.

"Yeah, but I know better than to stop you. Think of me as your muscle."

"Isn't that my job?" Jet asked. Then he started laughing. "Okay I thought I might be able to hold it together longer than that. I think Vic's right. We've come pretty close to being hurt before."

I couldn't deny Vic was built to intimidate. Something about being a fireman gave him an air of competence. "Fine. But this time is different. George is here. I've learned my lesson."

Vic gave me a look that said, no you haven't.

"We're making the killer hope they can stop us, or take the evidence," I corrected. "Desperate enough to make a mistake. Not enough to go on a killing spree."

George was leaning against the wall arms crossed. I appreciate that he hadn't told us to leave it to the police. Maybe I wasn't the only one who'd learned a lesson. "You're talking about deliberately provoking a murderer who's already killed once."

"It doesn't matter," Kashvi said. "This is a trap. We're not trying to be heroes. We set them up, you arrest them."

"I'm not sold on this plan," George said. "But you'll do it anyway. So if you won't act like normal civilians, I have to keep you from getting killed."

The phrasing hit me wrong. Normal citizens. Like he forgot we solved cases before. It was getting harder to ignore his attitude. Bad enough when he was on the job, but it was bleeding into our dates. "Do you have a suspect? A reasonable one? Every person we talked to so far isn't the killing type."

"I said I listen not share details on an active case," he snapped. "Let's get this plan lined up."

I took that as a no. "We understand that it's risky." Why wasn't anyone else arguing our side?

"I don't think you do." He cut me off, frustration bleeding through. "You run a diner, Eliza. You've been really lucky in the past. It won't last."

The room went very quiet.

"George," Vic said. His tone stayed even. "She knows what she's doing. We'll be there."

"Does she?" George swung toward him.

Vic didn't rise to the bait. "I'm listening to her plan because she's intelligent enough to have one. You might try the same."

George's jaw tightened. He looked back at me, and I saw genuine fear there—fear for my safety, fear of losing me. But for him that meant control, not support.

"If you do this," he said, voice dropping, "you do it with full police protection. Official capacity. Which means you follow my lead and my orders."

"Your orders," I repeated, the words sounded wrong. I told myself to let it go. It wasn't the time to confront this behavior. I would do that when the killer was behind bars.

"For your safety." He stepped closer, lowering his voice. "Eliza, I won't lose you."

He was as vulnerable as I'd ever seen him, and part of me hurt at the raw emotion there. But another part—a part that had been growing—saw the cage those words built.

"What do you need?" Vic asked, pulling my attention away from George. "To do this safely, what support would help?"

The contrast was jarring. George telling me what I had to do. Vic asking what I needed.

"Communication," I said. I focused on the practical question. "A way to signal if something goes wrong. And people nearby who can respond fast."

"I can do that," Vic said. "Be the lookout. Let George know when to move in. So they can stay hidden."

"That's not good enough," George interjected. "She needs a wire."

"Stop," Kashvi cut in. "This can't be overt. We don't know who'll show up. I don't think the killer will come near us if there's obvious police presence."

"Then you don't do it at all." George's voice went hard again, the professional distance back. "As the investigating officer, I'm telling you this is too dangerous."

"As the investigating officer," Jet said, "you don't actually have authority to stop civilians from meeting in a public place to discuss private matters."

George's expression darkened. "Don't play lawyer with me."

"I'm not playing anything." Jet stood. "I'm pointing out that you're trying to use your badge to control a situation—and people—you're afraid of losing control over."

"I'm trying to keep her alive!"

"By taking away her choice," Vic said. His voice stayed level. "That's not protection, George."

"This is ridiculous." George turned back to me, desperation creeping into his voice. "I'm not arguing any longer. What's the plan?"

Kashvi handed out the notes we'd made earlier. "We'll do it in public. Vic and Eliza can be having lunch at the festival. The last day. Lots of people around. George, you and Denise can be nearby. Jet and I will sit at a table close by. I've found something that looks like Amalia's notebook. It will be on the table."

"The community center," I said. "Tomorrow afternoon, around three. The last tastings will happen so everyone has an excuse to be there."

"Martha and Mrs. Waverly have agreed to gossip the details about," Kashvi said. "By lunch everyone in the area will know you're in possession of the book."

George nodded as he read. “No one eats or drinks anything.”

“No kidding,” I said.

“I’m guessing we’ll have a few visitors to our table, but I’ll figure out a signal when we know we have the killer.” Vic said the words directly to George. “Eliza’s safety comes first. It’s up to the cops to prove we’re right or wrong.”

“We only get one shot at this,” Jet said. “If we pick the wrong one, there’s nothing else to use as bait.”

“Don’t worry about that,” George said. “We have other ways of finding killers. I suppose this one is fast, at least.”

We spent the next twenty minutes mapping out contingencies: what if the killer didn’t take our bait? What if some other civilian sat with us? Everything we could come up with as worst-case scenarios.

“I don’t think we can be more prepared,” I said when the ideas petered out.

“I’ll do a walk through of the venue,” Vic said. “Fire inspection. No one will get in my way. I can figure out the best place for us to sit.”

“Thank you,” I said, and meant it for more than just the tactical support.

He understood. I saw it in his eyes. “That’s what partners do.”

Partners. Not protector and protected. Not authority and civilian. Partners.

After Vic gave me a quick kiss on the cheek. Jet retreated to help Kashvi close up the bookstore. George just grunted a goodbye and went to talk to his team.

I sat for a moment to review the plan one more time. This case was going to be over tomorrow. We hadn’t mentioned our suspicions to Vic or George about who we thought might show up; our new suspects, Knox, Amos, and Cleo.

My phone buzzed. A text from George: *I still think this is a mistake. But I'll have officers nearby. Please be careful.*

I stared at the message for a long moment before typing back: *Thank you.*

21

Knox's text came through at nine-thirty the next morning while I flipped *sopaipillas* for the breakfast crowd.

Got your message about the notebook pages. When can we meet? This is important—need to discuss protecting Aunt Amalia's legacy and family reputation.

I wiped cinnamon sugar from my phone screen. Suspect number one on the line. I sent a text back to have him meet at the agreed location and time. Then I use the group text to let everyone know.

For the rest of the morning I put my energy into serving my diners. Jacquie in the kitchen, Will and Lola serving and bussing. I walked around with a full carafe of coffee, simply enjoying the normalcy.

A few people tried to get details about the investigation, but I sidestepped the questions and moved on.

Birdie wandered past the window with her phone raised. Recording content. I saw Alistair hurrying toward Dunes Cafe, back in town after his mysterious appointment. To be honest, as much as his drama was tiring, I did miss him busting in and announcing some imagined outrage. I guess you get your fun wherever it came from.

Around ten-thirty, George walked in. Even in his off duty outfit of jeans and a Nueva Vida Rocks! t-shirt, he looked like a cop.

"Collett is setting up. Nothing from Cleo?" he asked. I wasn't sure what he felt. I mean we'd had an argument last night in front of an audience. But today his attitude was all business, and just a little cold.

"Coffee?" I asked, deciding I wouldn't poke at the emotions.

"Please." He accepted it with a tired smile. "Don't worry. I'm not going to try to talk you out of it. I've realized you won't give in."

It sounded like a decision that included more than just this trap. "Thanks."

"Detective Collett will be in civvies with another officer. She'll pretend to be on a date," George said. "I'll be mobile. He's probably going to run, so please don't chase him."

"I didn't expect him to cave like the last case," I said. "What did you and Vic come up with for a signal to arrest Knox?"

"It could be... I was going to say it might not be Knox. But I guess if we haven't heard from Cleo yet, she'd not biting." He drank his coffee. "Or she's planning another way to take the notebook back." He looked over his shoulder. "Vic is going to stand up. Hard to miss, and easy to explain."

"Won't you need the notebook for evidence?"

George looked at me over the rim of his mug and raised an eyebrow. It took me a moment to realize what he was waiting for. "I forgot. We don't have it. That's good, right? I bought my own trap so it was a solid plan?"

"She'll go through legal channels. If we get Knox today, I'll let her know we lied." He gestured for a refill.

"Thank you," I said. "For trusting us to do this. I know you don't want us in danger."

"I can't do anything else. Like I told the sheriff when I updated him, it's better to be involved, than to deal with the aftermath. You're all taking precautions," he said. "Even with a badge, confronting a killer is never actually safe."

OUR TABLE WAS in the middle of the designated eating area. The community center was set up much like a food court in a mall. Just with more variety and higher quality. Vic and I had sodas and nachos on the table but neither of us were eating. Detective Collett and her 'date' were sitting two tables away. Jet was walking past the booths as if he was trying to decide what to buy and Kashvi had taken a table just the other side of Denise. George stood near the entrance, another man beside him engaged in conversation.

I grabbed Vic's arm and said, "don't look now, but why is your uncle here?"

Vic grinned and put his hand on mine. "Uncle Brad decided he didn't want to miss the fun. George said he could use someone as cover. He'll make sure uncle Brad is safe."

Vic's uncle was the epitome of irascible. He was also happy to share an opinion whether you wanted it or not. And he was determined to find Vic a wife. "Let's hope Knox is either not guilty, or not willing to trample an old man to escape."

"Think he'll show?" Vic asked while pretending to be absorbed by my company, like a real date.

"He'll show," I said. "He needs to know what we found.

And I think the book contains something about his background too."

At three o'clock, Knox appeared at the entrance. He didn't notice George or Brad. His attention was all on me. He stuffed his hands in his pocket and walked toward our table. He looked worse than at our last meeting—dark circles, uncombed hair. There was something weighing heavily on him.

"Eliza," he said. "Thanks for meeting with me."

"Of course," I said. "Have a seat. This is Vic Simons."

"Your boyfriend?"

Vic squeezed my hand and said, "let's not do labels. I'm just a friend."

"So," Knox said. "Is it Amalia's notebook? Where did you find it?"

I looked at him and saw a man who was desperate to end a situation. Had he pretended to love his aunt all these years?

"What do you think she wrote?" I asked. I mean, I hadn't thought ahead enough to make something up.

"She had everyone's secrets in there," he said. "She called it her insurance policy. I don't know anything else."

"What are you planning to do with it?" Vic asked.

Knox looked at me when he answered. "Burn it. I loved my aunt, but she was poison. I guess someone else thought so, too. If I destroy it a lot of people will be happy."

I waited. This was the moment—I felt it in how he held himself, in the grief filling his eyes.

"I loved her," he said. "My whole life, Aunt Amalia was the one who saw me. When my parents were busy with the business, she took me to museums. Taught me about light and shadow."

"She meant the world to you."

"Everything." His voice cracked. "That's what makes it —" He pressed his palms on the table. "I tried everything else first. You have to understand that. I spent months looking for another way."

My pulse jumped, but I kept my voice level. "Another way to what?"

"To protect my father." The words were almost a whisper. "Five years ago, he stole from her. Not a lot at first—just enough to cover business expenses he didn't want tracked. But it grew. By the time he died, it was close to half a million."

I set down my mug. "Amalia found out."

"She hired a forensic accountant, documented everything." Knox's laugh was bitter. "Told my mom she had a choice. Pay the money back or sign over the control of the family trust. Cut us off from our payments until she decided the money had been paid back."

Every story about the real Amalia made me understand why she was dead. "What did your mother decide?"

"She's been putting off the decision," Knox picked up a napkin from the stack beside our nachos and started shredding it. "I told her to give Amalia the trust, but it's not up to me. I can make my own way. My sister is still in university, she relies on the trust for her education. My brother needs it to pay for my nephew's treatments."

"So why did Amalia have to die now?" Vic asked. I appreciated him bring us back to the line of conversation that might result in a confession.

"Aunt Amalia said she was tired of waiting. That after this event she was considering option three." He finished with the first napkin and selected another. "She was going to prove my mom had colluded. I don't know if any of it was true, but I didn't want my mom to go to jail."

Would that be enough? I couldn't glance at Detective Collett and give away her presence. I needed more. "So her death was convenient?"

"She'd already prepared the report—everything documented, copies for the DA." He met my eyes, and the pain I saw in them almost made me forgive him.

Only almost. He'd poisoned his aunt to hide the truth, not to prevent her lying about his dad. "Did you try to change her mind?"

"I begged her." His voice got louder. "Explained what it would do to him, to all of us. The family meant her too. She'd changed her name to Amalia Limonete for her brand. Norma Thorne wasn't high-end enough to be an important food critic."

I felt a wave of relief that the thing I loved to do, cooking in a diner, didn't come with brand expectations. Knox had a point. If Amalia went ahead with her threats, all it would take was one of her relatives to reveal her name, and she'd be embroiled in the scandal too.

"She wouldn't budge," he said as he reached for the third napkin to reduce to a pile of shreds. "She said principles without consequences weren't principles at all. I couldn't let her ruin everything."

Vic patted my hand, and I let him take over, hoping he'd get a real confession from Knox. "How long did you plan it?"

He flinched. "It didn't take long. Once I made the decision, everything came together."

"Eliza!" Alistair stormed over from the entrance.

Just as we were about to get a full confession. I take back the thought that life was duller without his theatrics.

"Oh, hello Detective Collett. I noticed your partner at the doorway." Alistair pointed at George like his words hadn't done enough. "Are you on the trail of the killer? I heard all about the investigation when I returned from New York. Have I mentioned I was talking to an investor about franchising?"

I couldn't answer him because I was horrified at Knox's reaction. His face was ashen and his attention flicked between George and Denise.

"Perhaps later," I said. I was interested how his meeting turned out because I couldn't imagine why anyone would want to duplicate Dunes and it's 1980s menu.

"I have to go," Knox said. He pushed himself erect. "I can't believe I fell for this. I needed that notebook to finish the job."

I reached for him, hoping to convince him it was better to stay. Vic stood. Knox pushed his chair back and jerked his arm away.

"Knox Thorne, you are under arrest for murder." Denise and her companion rose to stop him from running.

I saw George approaching from the entrance.

Knox sprinted in the opposite direction until he was past George.

He turned and ran for the exit.

Brad stepped in his way and kicked Knox's feet out from under him.

22

The morning after Knox's arrest, I opened EB Eats to find half the town waiting outside. News had traveled through Nueva Vida overnight, and everyone wanted the official version of what happened at the Festival Fairgrounds.

I unlocked the door at six instead of seven, knowing there was no point in delaying. Within minutes, every table was full, and I couldn't make the coffee fast enough.

"I heard the nephew did it," Mrs. Waverly said from her usual corner booth. "That nice photography boy. Never trust a man who spends too much time in a darkroom."

"He's not in a darkroom, Mrs. Waverly," Martha Hendricks said from the next table. "Photography's all digital now."

"Even worse. Digital things are suspicious."

I was saved from having to comment by George walking through the door, followed by Detective Collett. They both looked tired but satisfied.

"Morning, Eliza," George said, sliding onto a stool at the counter. "Got time to talk?"

"Let's go back to the alley," I said pointing with my elbow as I filled another mug. "It will be tight with three of us, but we'll have some privacy."

We stood next to the patio table I'd put out for staff breaks.

"First things first," George said. "Knox Thorne was formally charged this morning with first-degree murder. His lawyer's working on a plea arrangement, but he won't get much of a deal."

"Preliminary hearing in about three weeks," Detective Collett said. "Then it depends on whether he takes the plea or goes to trial. Based on his cooperation so far, I'd bet on the plea."

"You got a real confession?" I asked, though I knew they must have if there were lawyers involved. George wouldn't be here with that satisfied look otherwise.

"He told us every detail." George said. "The poison was on the spoon. He switched it in the confusion when she collapsed."

"Did you find the notebook?" I asked. "I hate to think it's out there ready to be used for blackmail."

"Keiko Nakamura handed it in this morning," Denise said. "There are a few pages missing, so she must have removed any mention of her activities. Since it's not part of the investigation, it forms part of her estate. Up to the heirs what happens."

"I hope they burn it," I said. "So it's over?"

"Its not that easy," George said. "You'll have to testify if the judge wants more details, or the deal isn't good enough."

After they left, I called Kashvi and we agreed to get together in The Open Page to clear the murder board and talk about the results that evening.

"That was intense," Anthone said when I passed

through the kitchen. I guess we should have closed the door while we talked. "I mean, I knew Knox confessed, but hearing all the details..."

"Yeah," I agreed. "It seems like every killer we meet has a real justification in their minds. The idea that murder isn't the only solution seems completely alien to them."

"Is it wrong that I kind of understand?" he said. "What Amalia did to those people—"

"Was cruel and wrong," I finished the thought for him. "But murder is still murder."

"I know." Jet leaned against the door frame. "It's just hard, you know? Understanding why someone did something terrible but also knowing they have to face consequences."

I left Will and Jacquie to close the diner and headed over to The Open page at six with a takeout bag of grilled cheese sandwiches. I never planned to solve murders, but this ritual always made me feel like we were officially done. I sent a little prayer out to the universe that no one else would need us to solve their death. Then I grimaced at the idea I'd done the opposite and attracted more. Maybe we should make the Detective Club official.

"What do you want to do first," Kashvi asked. "Eat, clear the board, talk?"

"I think I'd be happier talking and eating without looking at the mess we made," Jet said. "All that work and we didn't have the right name until almost too late."

We didn't have much to take down, but the pile of notes on the floor waited for us. Kashvi set the table while Jet and I dumped the papers and string in the recycle box. I grabbed a whiteboard eraser and cleared off the random writing.

It did feel lighter in the room without the investigation

splashed over the wall. Jet went to the tiny fridge and brought out beers for each of us. I didn't feel bad about drinking because we all lived in walking distance.

"I heard from Cleo," Kashvi said. "She's going to try the influencer world."

"For food?" I asked. She wouldn't follow in Amalia's footsteps, surely.

"True crime," Jet said on a laugh. "It's hot right now, and she has a copy of the notebook apparently. The idea is to talk to the victims and get a different view of crimes."

"I don't know if the people in her book will want to talk about it," I said.

"Felix is already scheduled," Jet said. "He didn't hesitate apparently. Wants to set the record straight about what they've done to fix what his dad did."

So maybe some good would come from Amalia's death.

I finished my sandwich and took a swig of beer. "I talked to George before I came."

"More details?" Kashvi asked and then she looked at me. "Oh, the talk."

"What talk?" Jet asked.

"About our relationship," I said. "I didn't want this to linger and turn into bitterness. I want to have a friend not a broken hearted enemy."

"It's not always possible," Jet said. "I've had various talks. Now I'm with Kashvi, I hope never to have one again."

"And you're really happy the other relationships were over, right?" Kashvi said with a mock glare.

"Yes, obviously I'm ecstatic that I was available to be swept off my feet."

"Did he take it okay?" Kashvi asked.

"Well sort of. I told him how I felt about being protected

so much. I said I liked him but we couldn't be anything except friends. He didn't really say anything."

"Maybe when he sees you out with Vic he'll believe it?" Jet said. "Sometime we need a bit more evidence for the truth to settle in."

"I'm not exactly choosing Vic either. I like being a free agent for now." I really didn't want George to think he lost me to someone he already disliked.

23

When I arrived at the diner the next morning, ready to start the grill for Jacquie and get the prep underway, Anthone was waiting for me, a pot of coffee already brewed and a plate of blueberry muffins on the counter.

"I need some advice," he said.

"So," I said, peeling the paper away from the warm muffin. "You've finally decided to leave me?"

"Sort of." Anthone filled our mugs. "I think I have to do it now before I get too comfortable. The time I spent doing catering with Bernie was like running a small restaurant. I learned the business side. Now, I think I've decided what kind of food I'll serve."

"I hate to say it, but you are ready. I'll always be a phone call away, if you need anything," I tried to keep my voice light, but I would really miss him.

"I'm opening a vegan bistro right here in Nueva Vida," he said. "Nothing big, but no one else is doing it and vegan is really interesting."

"I was afraid you were off to Albuquerque." I bit into the

muffin to stop myself from crying. "I didn't know you were interested in vegan."

"That muffin is one of my new offerings." He handed me a pot of something that looked like butter. "All oil based. I've also started researching a product I can market. Not sure what yet."

"When are you leaving?" I already knew Cassidey would take more hours so we wouldn't be stuck.

"It'll take a month," he said. "If you let me stay until then. I'll be your competition after all."

"Anthone as long as you don't serve bacon and eggs, or chili with meat, I'm fine." I almost choked on the muffin when he pulled a horrified face like the idea of meat was so awful.

My shift was ending when George came to the diner that afternoon. He was in his civilian clothes and looked tired as usual. I hated the idea that my ending our budding romance got in the way of him sleeping.

"Eliza," he said, nodding to me. "Could we talk? Won't take long."

I followed him to a quiet booth away from prying ears. He placed his messenger bag on the table and flipped it open.

"I thought about what you said yesterday," he said after waving Lissa away when she offered coffee. "About needing different things from a relationship."

"George—"

"Let me finish." He smiled, but it just made him look sadder. "You were right. I was trying to protect you, which is what I do—it's who I am as a cop and probably as a person. But you don't need protection."

There was definitely another shoe about to drop. "I appreciate you understanding that."

"I'm trying to and I promise I can be civil. It might take a while to get back to friendly." He pulled a handful of papers from the bag. "In an effort to start on that path, I brought the statements for you to sign."

"Instead of demanding I come to the station? That's exactly what a friend would do." He didn't react to my encouragement.

"Read and sign at the bottom. The first one is from the night of the murder and the second one is when we caught him."

Okay, maybe we were stuck in civil for now. I read the statements and signed the bottom of both. It was odd to see the events laid out so clinically. "The facts are right and I don't think anything is missing."

"Thanks, I still have a mountain of paperwork but it's in the hands of the lawyers now." He tucked the statements into the bag and slid out of the booth. "Try not to get involved in any future investigations, Eliza. I'm not sure I can keep you out of jail the next time."

I smiled and said I'd see him around. No way was I making any promises.

WANT MORE

Ready for another mystery at EB Eats?
Murder crashes the mayoral election in A Dead Heat—and this time, the killer might be running Nueva Vida.
Use the QR code to Get your copy of A Dead Heat now!

FREE BOOK

Use the QR code to claim your copy of Burned by BLT when you sign up for my newsletter learn how Eliza became so determined to clear her name.

REVIEW

~

If you enjoyed reading A Bitter End please consider helping other readers to find the story by using the QR code to leave a review.

ALSO BY PRINT

For more books by Poppy Bridgeman

scan the QR code below.

ABOUT POPPY BRIDGEMAN

Hi, I'm Poppy Bridgeman, the cozy mystery alter ego of Canadian author P A Wilson. Poppy was "born" because sometimes stories need a gentler touch—with a little magic, a dash of humor, and plenty of sleuthing spirit.

As Poppy, I write the *Witch of Henbane Island* series (where witches and festivals collide with mysteries), the *EB Eats Culinary Mysteries* (a small-town diner, a determined heroine, and murder on the menu), and the *Pages & Paws Bookstore Mysteries* (a Devon bookshop, two mischievous corgis, and plenty of secrets tucked between the shelves).

When I'm not tangled in my characters' escapades, I'm happily tangled in yarn—I knit, weave, and doodle in sketchbooks between writing sessions. I also love to travel, finding inspiration for charming settings, quirky characters, and suspicious strangers wherever I go.

Home base is the Vancouver area, where I juggle writing as both Poppy and P A Wilson. Whichever name is on the cover, I'm always chasing the next story.

ACKNOWLEDGMENTS

Writing may look like a solitary pursuit, but I could never do this alone. I've been lucky to have support, encouragement, and inspiration from so many corners that it's impossible to thank everyone properly—but I'll try.

My writing groups keep me sharp and creative: The Vancouver Writers Social Group challenges me to see stories in new ways, The Royal City Literary Arts Society has given me the chance to learn from generous and talented writers, and The Other 11 Months group reminds me that words on the page are what really matter. My critique partners, with their sharp eyes and honest feedback, make sure each story is the best version it can be.

And of course, my heartfelt thanks to my beta readers. You catch the wobbly bits, cheer for the good ones, and remind me that these stories aren't just mine—they're meant for you, my readers.

www.ingramcontent.com/pod-product-compliance
Lightning Source LLC
La Vergne TN
LVHW030920080826
845145LV00013B/2981

* 9 7 8 1 9 9 0 5 0 9 8 3 4 *